TWO'S COMPANY,
THREE'S DEADLY

Holden opened his eyes. The FLNA woman was standing over him, bringing the muzzle of her pistol down toward his chest. "Kiss your—"

"You kiss yours, honey!" It was Rosie's voice. Rosie's right foot snaked out, impacting the woman in the right ribcage, sending her sprawling.

Holden was up. The remaining man charged toward them, firing his assault rifle. Holden punched the Desert Eagle toward the man and fired, then again and again. All three shots connected, the assault rifle spraying out across the deck plates. The hit body went twisting and fell.

Holden looked to his left. Rosie Shepherd's left hand was locked to the woman's gunhand wrist, the pistol discharging into the air. Rosie took a half-step back. Her tiny right fist straight-armed into the woman's windpipe.

The gun fell from dead fingers.

"This time you saved my bacon," Holden grinned.

Rosie grinned back. "Let's get the hell out of here and then we can discuss repaying each other, huh?"

Other titles in the Defender Series:

JUSTICE DENIED

Jerry Ahern

A DELL BOOK

Published by
Dell Publishing
a division of
Bantam Doubleday Dell
Publishing Group, Inc.
666 Fifth Avenue
New York, New York 10103

ISBN: 0-440-20332-5

Printed in the United States of America
Published simultaneously in Canada

August 1989

10 9 8 7 6 5 4 3 2 1

For our buddy Sid Woodcock, who can do all the derring-do standing on his head because he's done it already. Best wishes . . .

CHAPTER 1

Sa'd ibn-Mu'adh, his knife clamped tight in his teeth, rose out of the water and clambered up the handlelike rungs set against the prow of the cutter, near to the anchor wells. Others rose from the water with him, while still others labored hand over hand along the underside of the gangplank. The men with him were expendable, of course, because they were unbelievers and they were in sufficient number that several of them could die and the mission could be carried out regardless.

He waited, his eyes level with the deck, as brackish seawater dripped from his heavy brows. He carefully watched a man with white cap over his blond hair and a pistol holstered at his side, just now turning around. Ibn-Mu'adh pushed himself up and flipped over the rail. The Coast Guardsman reached for his pistol. Ibn-Mu'adh raked his knife across the man's throat, bringing him down silently to the deck.

Warring against the Infidels was satisfying because there were no concerns of conscience. Not for him. By their very refusal to accept Islam, however, tacit that denial, they were condemned to the will of Satan. Yet among the many who called themselves Muslim, some were worse than the Infidels. Those who outwardly professed faith but inwardly rejected its teachings condemned themselves not only to Satan but to death. It

1

was insanity to believe that one who accepted the teachings of Islam should be constrained against striking down the enemies of Islam, by laws and covenants created by mere men. His taken name was a name of much history. Sa'd ibn-Mu'adh had stood against the Jews and aided the Prophet Muhammad in his struggles in the Battle of Badr.

But more days of historic glory lay ahead.

Ibn-Mu'adh took the dead man's pistol and moved along the deck. There was a groan of pain as another of the Coast Guardsmen was brought down by one of the American street punks who worked with ibn-Mu'adh.

Ibn-Mu'adh crouched beside the wheelhouse, waiting for more of the men to consolidate on the deck, and he found himself thinking of Dimitri Borsoi. Borsoi, though an Infidel, was a destroyer. Men like Borsoi would make the Great Satan collapse of its own weight, bringing on the day of justice all the sooner. . . .

The yacht belonging to Tom Ashbrooke's friend, Demosthenes Dimitropoulous, was stopped. David Holden sat bolt upright in bed and Rosie Shepherd sat up beside him. There was a Walther P-5 9mm that Dimitropoulous the smuggler had loaned him stashed on the floor just under the bed, and Holden reached down for it. The light through the porthole was a diffused gray and Holden was unable clearly to see the luminous face of his wristwatch. It was too light for the luminosity and too dark to be able to read the hands without it. "What time is it?"

"The boat stopped."

"Check the time."

Rosie Shepherd rolled over to her right, both her wristwatches in a niche within the shelved headboard. She took down the Timex Ironman. Holden smiled. "Iron woman" might perhaps be a better name, he thought. She was as tough a fighter as any man he'd ever met, a warm, gentle lover, and to him no less the epitome of womanhood than his late wife, Elizabeth (Tom Ashbrooke's daughter and the mother of Holden's three now dead children), had been. Elizabeth had known how to handle the little gun he'd given her, although she'd resented carrying it because it made her purse too heavy. It still angered him that the authorities had been irrationally obsessed with her gun to the exclusion of finding her killers in the aftermath of her death. He doubted she could have used it against another human being. Yet, in her own way, she was a fighter. She had fought to raise their children to be decent, sensitive human beings, to be concerned for others as well as for themselves, and had fought to make their home and their lives happy. She knew no martial art, used a knife only in the kitchen or to spread more peanut butter on bread for the children's picnic lunches.

He looked at Rosie Shepherd. The more deeply he loved Rosie, an ex-cop with a mouth that could have made a sailor blush, the more profoundly he realized that despite Rosie and Elizabeth's glaring dissimilarities, they were in other ways very much alike.

"It's six-fifteen, David."

Her inexpensive wristwatch could be illuminated by merely pushing a button. His watch, a Rolex, was useless to him at the moment. When he listened very hard, he could hear it tick and faintly beyond that the lapping of water against the hull and near to him breathing.

He shrugged and, handing her the P-5, reached into the headboard shelf nearest him for the Desert Eagle. This Desert Eagle .44 wasn't the one Rufus Burroughs had carried until his death, which David Holden had inherited along with the mantle of leadership for the Metro Patriots in the fight against the Front for the Liberation of North America. But, in a way, this Desert Eagle meant as much to him. When Rosie had joined Tom Ashbrooke and the small group of Israeli commandos, and had risked her life to come and rescue him from the Peruvian drug lords who financed the FLNA, she'd brought the gun for him.

There was no need to check the chamber. It was loaded and hadn't been out of his sight since he'd checked it just before they'd gone to bed around ten P.M.

"I hope nothing's gone wrong," Rosie almost whispered. "I need a shower. That's your fault." She laughed softly, but the laugh sounded forced.

He leaned toward her and kissed her lightly, quickly, on the mouth, telling her, "I hope you'll need a shower every morning in your life because of me." Holden swung his legs over the side of the bed and stood up. Naked, the Desert Eagle in his right fist, he crossed the cabin floor to the nearest porthole. There were two cabins belowdecks in the yacht's forward section, the other occupied by Demosthenes Dimitropoulous himself.

Through the porthole David Holden could see a

Coast Guard cutter perhaps two hundred yards off the port bow. "Shit," Holden hissed through his teeth.

The bedside phone rang; in the next instant Rosie asked him, "Should I answer it?"

"Probably Dimitropoulous. Answer it," Holden told her. He walked back toward the bed and stood beside it, watching her as she spoke into the receiver.

"Hello?"

He crossed the cabin to the closet. Over the chair near it were his pants. Their bags, packed the night before, were just inside the closet door. Atop his bag were a fresh change of underpants, socks, and a handkerchief. He skinned into the underpants and socks.

Rosie hung up the telephone. "We should meet him on the deck as soon as we can. I should dress up and you should try looking like a seaman. Trouble. Coasties. They ordered us to heave to or something." She stood up and the sheet that had been pulled up over her breasts fell away. Rosie looked very pretty naked, Holden thought suddenly. Her breasts weren't the largest, but they were well shaped and matched her leggy, almost lithe look. She tossed her auburn hair back and started for the head. . . .

The Coast Guard cutter was very close. Two motorized skiffs were being lowered into the water and the covering on the deck gun was removed.

"I do not like this very much at all. Do you know how many times I have been stopped by Coast Guard vessels in all my years as an importer? Ha! Never two launches. And still in international waters!" Demosthenes Dimitropoulous stood in the bow pulpit, scratching his close-cropped beard, which was tinged with red and silver, as his salt-and-pepper gray hair, less colorful than his beard, blew in the salt spray. The yacht, when in full sail, reminded Holden of one of the great sailing ships of the nineteenth century, nearly that long and that wide abeam, multimasted and exuding power. But now she was seesawing badly against the swells with all sails furled and her engines shut down.

"How long would it take to restart the engines?" Rosie asked him, raising her voice over the keening of the wind. With the back of her left hand she pushed her hair back from her face (a useless gesture with the wind blowing as strongly as it was and her hair unbound).

"The question is academic. With the two of you aboard," Dimitropoulous said, smiling, "I would never have stopped if there had been a chance to outrun them. This smells very badly"—and he laid his left forefinger alongside his nose like Santa Claus from the Christmas poem. "I would have ordered the guns thrown over the side, but I somehow felt we would need them."

David Holden found little reassurance in the Desert Eagle that was stuffed inside his trouser band underneath his borrowed windbreaker. Eight .44 Magnum rounds were a poor hedge against a deck-mounted machine-gun.

"I will say that you, Miss Shepherd, are my inamorata of the moment." And Dimitropoulous looked down at Rosie and smiled. "What a pleasant thought that would be were it true." Rosie blushed, one hand fighting to keep her hair back from her face, the other to keep her nearly ankle-length khaki-colored full skirt under control. He looked at David Holden. "Give me a salute in a minute. They are watching us, of course. Then go below and join Captain Selonikas as if you were a member of the crew. There are UZIs and other weapons. If they insist on a detailed search, you may need them."

"Coast Guardsmen aren't my enemies. And they aren't yours either. We have to think of another way out of this," Holden said quickly.

"Well, my friend, you are right, of course, but if these were real Coast Guardsmen acting with legal authorization, they wouldn't be here and they wouldn't be sending over those men with nonissue weapons—look." And he nodded toward the approaching launches. Holden could see submachine guns. He didn't know what was issue these days for the Coast Guard and trusted that Dimitropoulous probably did. At any event, they looked like UZIs. "In the final analysis, my friends," Dimitropoulous concluded, "they are either pirates or they have been sent by your nemesis in the FLNA. Because that is as genuine a cutter as I have seen."

A crewman approached, gave a nonmilitary salute, and handed Dimitropoulous a note. Dimitropoulous glanced over the sheet of yellow paper, then began to summarize it. "This radio message is from the United States Coast Guard, warning all vessels navigating in this area to be on the lookout for"—and he glanced over his shoulder and toward the cutter—"for that. There is reason to suspect the vessel's crew was killed, since several bodies were found where she was moored.

Bodies of the guards posted on the dock, I would surmise."

Rosie Shepherd muttered something half lost on the wind, but it sounded like the word *shit*.

Holden eyed the launches. "We can't call the real Coast Guard, because they'd nail us."

"And, in international waters, they have no authority. We could attempt to summon your United States Navy, but by the time authorization was given, the battle would be over at any event. Go below and wait. The battle will be soon, but I wanted it on my terms."

Holden took a step back, rendered a smart handsalute, and started aft. The Desert Eagle rested heavily against his abdomen. He knew they weren't pirates. Somehow word of his and Rosie's return to the United States had leaked. They were FLNA, come to kill him and Rosie and everyone aboard.

Holden quickened his pace. There were some things he'd learned as a SEAL which, if Dimitropoulous had the necessary items aboard, might even the odds a little.

David Holden looked over his shoulder toward the Cutter's deck gun.

As soon as he reached the forward companionway steps and was out of sight from the launches, he started to run.

CHAPTER 2

"Soon, within the next hour, one of the chief obstacles to our success will be removed forever. With his death and with the restrictions on the activities and rights of these Americans which come almost hourly from the White House and from Congress, the climate is perfect for escalating the most important element of our campaign."

Dimitri Borsoi's legs hurt, but he stood on his crutches anyway. Assembled before him, sitting on folding chairs in the metal Butler Building, which was the size of an American basketball court, were the men whose charge it would be to carry out this next and possibly final stage in the destruction of the United States. He cleared his throat, then continued. "Terror is the one indispensable commodity. With terror as our weapon and a government disarming its people, estranging itself from the governed, the people of this pig nation will be divided into warring factions, destroying themselves. I mean ultimate terror. We have periodically used terror, but now we shall use it to its fullest advantage. No home will be safe. No child walking home from school, no woman in her kitchen, no man at his work. Death will find them, but death of the most violent sort. The average American family, a man and woman and their two point three children, sit at home watching television, a comedy, perhaps. Your men will strike at random and break in upon this typical American family. Shoot the man. Rape the woman and girl, sodomize the boy, hack the bodies to pieces with machetes. Leave them until the smell of them attracts someone and suddenly another random act of demoralizing terror is broadcast on the seven o'clock news. But by that time another man and woman and two point whatever children will be dead, and another and another and another."

CHAPTER 3

There had been so many resigned commissions that President Makowski, as Commander-in-Chief, had suspended the traditional officers' prerogative and would accept no more resignations. But Arlo Wentworth's lieutenant had reported to sick call, the schmuck.

The van stopped and Wentworth gave a quick glance to his men, then wrenched open the sliding door on the passenger side and jumped, shouting, "Let's go!"

It was like Vietnam, like exiting a helicopter, with the enemy out there in the jungle waiting to open fire. It was exciting and it beat working reduced shifts at the convenience store.

He ran, crouched, just as if helicopter rotor blades were sweeping lethally overhead.

It wasn't hot, as Vietnam had been, but he sweated just the same, his men around him in a ragged wedge formation as they stormed up the driveway.

. . . *by Executive Order 128946, the right to possession of firearms of any type or description capable of being concealed upon the body or possessed of a detachable box-type magazine, whether handgun, rifle, or shotgun, shall be proscribed for the duration of the current crisis. All persons, corporate entities, and sundry others possessed of same proscribed weapons are compelled by law to surrender these in exchange for*

11

receipt for same, said value or renumeration to be prescribed by law.

Arlo Wentworth nearly had it memorized and it had only been in effect for three days.

They ran along the driveway of 138 Maplewood Drive.

There was a plastic big-wheeled tricycle in the middle of the driveway and Wentworth kicked it away. "Search that station wagon! Don't forget!"

"Yes, Sergeant!"

Wentworth, his M-16 at high port, reached the front door, stopped, and knocked.

There was a doorbell. He rang it.

Two of his men flanked him, the others surrounding the house.

The door opened.

The woman standing in the partially open doorway screamed and tried to close the door. Wentworth stomped his combat booted foot between the door and the jam. "Mrs. Cunningham?"

"Yes—but who—"

"Master Sergeant Arlo Wentworth, ma'am, National Guard detailed to enforcement duties for Executive Order 128946, to whit—"

"Pete!" The woman screamed and tried to close the door. Wentworth slammed the butt of his M-16 against it, breaking one of the small stained-glass panels, then shouldered his way past her. "Pete!"

"We have no intention of harming anyone, ma'am. We have information that leads us to believe you and your husband are concealing arms proscribed by Executive Order 128946, as reported to the Task Force on Domestic Violence by a concerned citizen."

"Pete! Pete! Pete!"

She screamed and started to run. Corporal Wisniewski blocked the doorway. "I wouldn't ma'am."

A man appeared in the kitchen doorway. Arlo Wentworth dropped into a crouch, leveling the M-16 at the man's chest without thinking. "Are you Mr. Peter Harrison Cunningham, sir?"

"What the fuck you doin' to my wife!" The man charged him and Arlo Wentworth had no choice. He was empowered by Executive Order 128946 to use whatever force might be necessary. A horizontal buttstroke with the M-16—the gun rattled disappointingly—laid out Mr. Peter Harrison Cunningham, flopping him back half onto the couch, a vase with dried flowers in it tumbling off the coffee table and shattering on the floor.

"Ma'am—"

She was already running across the room and dropped to her knees, her dress billowing out around her legs. Her husband's head was in her hands, then against her lap. She looked up at Wentworth, screaming, "You bastard! You dirty—"

"Ma'am, I could arrest you for using such abusive language, but I won't if you'll stop."

Wentworth dropped to one knee beside Mr. Peter Harrison Cunningham. Mr. Peter Harrison Cunningham was unconscious, blood dribbling out of the left corner of his mouth and all around his lower lip. Wentworth wore gloves, alert to the insidious dangers of acquired immune deficiency syndrome. Never hit a man in the mouth unless you are wearing gloves. Split his lip and split your knuckles and you might be setting yourself up for the big one.

"Search the house. Our information indicates that there are several dozen automatic weapons secreted here."

"That's a lie!" She was sobbing now, rocking Mr. Peter Harrison Cunningham's head back and forth in her arms. "Pete has a handgun and some kind of shotgun and his father's deer rifle."

"I'm sorry, ma'am. We have to check the house and grounds. If we don't locate his weapons cache, there'll be a lot of explaining to do when we hand you over to the civil authorities. So you'd better help us find everything."

"I can show you where the three guns are!"

Wisniewski unslung his metals detector. The rest of Wentworth's men were coming in through the back door. Already he could hear cabinets being opened.

The house was nicely furnished.

"There's some metal in the wall here near the fireplace. Could be a secret panel, Sergeant," Wisniewski sang out.

"There's nothing back there! Please!"

It would be a shame what they might have to do to the wallpaper.

But contraband was contraband. "Get the ax out of the van."

"No!"

CHAPTER 4

Rose Shepherd felt Dimitropoulous's arm curl around her waist and she snuggled close against him, keeping her knees close together under her skirt because she had a Walther P-5 9mm lashed to the inside of her left thigh with the elastic waistband from a slip. When she moved, she could feel the pistol move a little. If it fell to the deck between her feet, it would be socially awkward, because the half-dozen men in Coast Guard uniforms who were crowding beside the ladder that led up from their motor launch to the deck of the yacht were all armed with UZIs.

The fake captain of the Coast Guard vessel actually looked and sounded quite genuine. "Mr. Dimitropoulous? Demosthenes Dimitropoulos?"

"If you know who I am, then you know who I am. What is the meaning of interrupting my voyage? I will remind you, these are international waters."

"We understand, sir, that you may be harboring notorious fugitives aboard this vessel." They knew, all right, she realized. She noticed the eyes of one of the men who was very foreign looking and a little older than the others. They never left her. She pulled her sweater closer around her. His eyes made her feel naked and colder than she had been.

"You are insane. And you have no authority here.

I demand that you disembark and let us continue our voyage."

"And just what is the exact nature of your voyage, sir?"

Dimitropoulous held her more tightly. "Pleasure, my young friend. You got us out of bed."

Rosie made a smile she didn't feel, the fingers of her right hand drifting fondlingly across Dimitropoulous's muscular chest.

They wanted to get permission to search the boat so they could get more of their men on deck before the shooting started, she realized.

She licked her lips. She'd forgotten to put on lipstick. . . .

David Holden came up over the gunwale of the cutter's squared-off aftersection, the Defender knife in his teeth. The plastique that Spiros Selonikas, the captain of Dimitropoulous's yacht, had given him was strapped to his back inside a waterproof bag inside an ordinary canvas teardrop-shaped rucksack. The rucksack felt as if it weighed a hundred pounds as he rolled over the handrail, his head beside the coaming as he came up in a crouch.

The water wasn't as cold as he'd thought it would be, it was colder. As he peered over the side, he could see the men from the second launch scrambling up the ladder alongside the yacht. In a few moments both boarding parties would be on deck. Then the shooting would start.

He could see Rosie and Dimitropoulous, snuggling

together like lovers amidships on the port side near the furled mainsheet.

Holden started moving forward along the starboard side of the cutter's superstructure.

A footfall.

Holden tucked back, hearing voices. His hand grabbed the deck rail and he vaulted over, his arms and shoulders screaming at him with momentary pain as he caught the full weight of his body.

He swung around, moving first his right hand, then his left, got down to deck level and hung there. The voices increased in loudness, then reached a peak, then dropped. He also heard the rattles of slings on weapons.

His eyes shifted to the Rolex Sea-dweller on his left wrist. He was taking too much time.

He started pulling himself up, slowly at first, eyes level with the sheer line. He then came up and over the gunwale.

He moved rapidly forward, reaching the after bulkhead of the superstructure. Presumably the men he had heard and several others, a dozen in all, were waiting on the port side, M-16's and UZIs ready. There was a boat winching down over the side.

Two men were at the deck gun. Holden guessed it was a .50 caliber, but he knew nothing about the Coast Guard's equipment.

He took the ladder up to the wheelhouse, where a solitary man stood. Holden took the knife from his teeth and charged toward him.

The man wheeled around, a Beretta 9mm in his right fist. Holden dropped to his left hand and scissored his legs, bringing the man down, no shot fired—yet. Holden threw himself on the man's back, the knife in Holden's right fist raking across the man's throat as Holden averted his eyes from the blood spray.

There was a P-5 in a waterproof sack inside his pack, but Holden took up the dead man's 92F instead, press-checking the slide to find there was a chambered round, leaving the safety off.

He moved to the main control console, slipping the pack off his shoulders. There were two separate blocks of plastique. He took the smaller one and set to work on the underside of the console, rigging the detonator into the electrical connects for the starboard throttle. . . .

All twelve men from the two launches were aboard the yacht now and the look in the dark eyes of the foreign-seeming man had changed.

Rosie Shepherd, taking short steps because of the gun on the inside of her left thigh, backed away, with Dimitropoulous moving beside her.

It was the foreign man who spoke. "You are the bitch American police officer Rose Shepherd, are you not?"

She felt Dimitropoulous's arm muscles tense and his hand left her waist. Then she took a half step forward. "You're in deep shit, fella." She didn't know what else to say as a follow-up but hoped she was right.

Captain Selonikas had about the same number of men, and unless he was a damned poor smuggler, he should have them in position to cut these guys down if they moved funny. She hoped.

The foreigner walked toward her, his right hand moving not at all, but his left hand snaking up before she could react and backhanding her across the face.

She let herself fall to the deck as Dimitropoulous started to move and the UZI nearest him started to swing toward him. Her left hand hitched her skirt nearly to her hips so she could clear it with the Walther as her right hand tore the pistol from the elastic tied around her thigh. She stabbed the P-5 toward the man who was about to shoot Dimitropoulous, the double-action pull just tightening to break as the man fired.

There was a burst from the UZI as her shot impacted him in the left side of the throat.

Dimitropoulous—

She rolled right across the deck, her skirt winding around her. Her legs—there hadn't been time for stockings either—felt the cold of the deck. A chunk of the decking blew out as another UZI was fired.

Rosie put a double tap into the chest of the man in the captain's uniform, his pistol on line with her face. She rolled, another UZI firing as the fake captain went down.

Dimitropoulous, the Greek smuggler, was alive. With a pistol in his right hand and his arm at full extension he was firing a P-5 identical to her own. One of the boarding party fired his UZI into the deck, sending splinters of decking flying everywhere. Rosie averted her eyes as she felt hands pulling her back by the shoulders. She twisted the pistol around to fire, heard Captain Selonikas's voice shouting something in Greek, and suddenly there was gunfire everywhere.

Her eyes met the eye of one of the sailors from the crew of the yacht.

Then she heard it, an explosion. . . .

David Holden swam with the Beretta in his right fist and his knife sheathed in a borrowed fabric scabbard that fit it marginally well. The ocean surface was sent seething up around him as the first explosion came. The second, smaller one came shortly after. He tucked down beneath the waves to protect himself.

Holden rolled one hundred eighty degrees, pushing up. Debris littered the water around him. Pieces of the cutter were still raining down as a fireball, black and orange, belched skyward.

He'd planted two charges, the first one rigged to the throttle in the event the cutter started to close with the yacht, the second one rigged on a timer set for four minutes. He glanced at his watch. The timer had been a few seconds off.

Holden looked toward the yacht. There was more gunfire from the deck now, the men in the third launch opening fire on the deck with their assault rifles and submachine guns.

Holden pushed up and dived below the surface, still holding to the Beretta pistol, moving toward the third launch. . . .

Rosie Shepherd crouched in the well for the companionway steps. The Walther, more or less half emptied anyway, had been swapped for a semiautomatic UZI carbine. The stock was folded out and her left forearm entwined in the sling.

Three sailors were with her. Dimitropoulous and two other men were near the mainmast. Five of the fake Coast Guardsmen, the foreign-looking one with the scary black eyes among them, were all the way aft.

Dimitropoulous shouted to her, "We have to rush them! They could plant explosives in the machinery spaces!"

She didn't quite know what machinery spaces were, but she believed him.

"You can cover us, Rosie!"

"Cover my ass!" And she was up, catching up her skirt from behind and pulling it forward between her legs and stuffing the hem into her waistband making improvised trousers.

She moved up the companionway steps to the level of the deck, peering over it with the UZI carbine at eye level beside her face.

She could see Dimitropoulous and the two sailors with him edging forward. Captain Selonikas and another man were crouched behind a built-in trunk that they kept rope in that was near the mainmast. They looked ready to move. She shouted, "Follow me!"

Once out of the well for the companionway steps, she ran along the main cabin top, keeping low, and stopped beside another set of companionway steps, licking her lips.

Gunfire blasted from the stern, tearing a chunk away from the ornamental woodwork surrounding the frame for the well into which the steps were set.

"Eat lead," she shrieked back, firing rapid semi-automatic bursts from the UZI carbine at her shoulder, chunks of trim from the cockpit moldings blowing off as her slugs impacted. Automatic weapons fire from a half-dozen men on a third launch impacted all around her, and she threw herself down the companionway steps. "Dammit!" She rearranged herself on the steps, restuffing the hem of her skirt into her waistband again, then punched the UZI over the rim of the well, firing forward, emptying half the magazine. She made a tactical change to a full magazine, then started up to deck level again.

Gunfire came from forward. Dimitropoulous shouted to her, "Stay down!"

Of course she didn't, but she kept low, firing toward the five men holding the position in the stern. She laid the long barrel of the carbine a few inches over the level of the deck and fired, hoping she'd catch a stray foot or leg. Where was David? She kept shooting. . . .

David Holden surfaced, gulped air, and looked around. The third launch was about twenty yards off, the men crouched behind her gunwales, firing toward the deck of the yacht. He looked to the yacht. There was a raging gun-battle there, but he couldn't tell who was winning.

He gulped air again and dived beneath the surface, using broad, easy strokes to conserve strength as he moved through the water toward the starboard quarter of the launch.

Everyone was looking forward—

The dark shape of the launch's hull loomed above him and Holden swam up to meet it.

There was a better than ninety percent chance the

ammunition in the liberated Beretta would still work, which meant there was a slightly less than ten percent chance he'd have no weapon except his knife.

His left hand grasped the transom and he pulled himself up, half out of the water. His right hand reached up as he looked forward.

The rattle of gunfire was almost deafeningly loud.

No one was watching him.

He eased over the transom, first with his left leg then with his right.

He held the Beretta muzzle down so any residual water in the barrel would drip out and there would be less chance of water forming a stoppage and bursting the barrel.

Maybe he had felt the subtle shift in the launch's draft, but whatever the reason the man farthest aft started slowly to turn around. Holden raised the Beretta, the safety already up and off, his left hand going for the haft of the Defender knife as his right first finger pulled the trigger.

His ears were alert for any strange sound as the Beretta fired that would indicate a stoppage or a problem with the cartridge. There was none, only a normal-sounding 9mm Parabellum pistol shot.

The man fell back, his assault rifle spraying upward.

Holden swung the Beretta's muzzle on line and fired as one of the other men turned toward him. A double tap into the chest and neck sent the man sprawling half over the gunwale.

Holden turned the Beretta on the others, firing it

out, shooting men in the back, in the rib cage, whatever was the best target.

The Beretta was empty.

One of the fake Coast Guardsmen was still moving, trying to raise his rifle.

David Holden fell on him with the butt of the pistol and with his knife. . . .

She was pinned down.

Rose Shepherd looked below her. Though a passenger on the yacht for better than nine days, she did not, despite its size, know every inch of the vessel but was familiar with most of it. She started down the steps, the crew's head at the base.

Her UZI at high port, she hugged to the bulkhead beside the free-standing drinking fountain that was bolted to the decking there.

Rose Shepherd looked right and left, licked her lips.

She reached to the waistband of her skirt, taking the last full magazine for the UZI carbine and exchanging it for the partially spent one already in place. Dropping to her knees behind the drinking fountain, she felt the wet carpeting against her skin.

Quickly she thumbed out cartridges from the least full of the other two magazines, emptying it, then inserted the loose rounds one at a time beneath the feed lips of the fuller of the two, her fingers hurting as she fought the magazine spring pressure. When the magazine was full, she took the six remaining loose rounds and reinserted them in the magazine that she'd just emptied.

She stuck the nearly empty magazine into the waistband of her skirt at the small of her back, the full one over her abdomen.

She tightened her grip on the UZI carbine, peered around the drinking fountain, and started aft.

Past the long table for the crew's quarters, she smelled something still cooking or more likely burning on the stove fresh on the air from the galley just forward of where she had come below. Next she came to the hanging lockers. Each locker door was a neat, clean green with a neatly stenciled name on it.

Beyond the lockers were berths. They were wide and looked comfortable. Dimitropoulous had told them that racing yachts had Spartan interiors, especially for the working crew; oftentimes several men used the same V-berth as they rotated on and off watch.

There were two automatic coffee makers, one with coffee and the other with plain hot water for men who wanted tea instead.

The coffee smelled good and reminded her that she hadn't had any breakfast.

Rose Shepherd kept moving, but very slowly. . . .

Ibn-Mu'adh crouched by the doorway of the portside aft stateroom, glancing inside.

Decadence was lewdly, almost proudly displayed.

He saw sheets of what looked to be fine linen on a bed that three or four could have slept comfortably upon, a television set, a videocassette recorder, a stereo, and books. Many of these latter, no doubt, were pernicious in the extreme. He could imagine what the capitalist smuggler pig Dimitropoulous provided for his guests to view and to read. Videotapes and picture books and magazines filled with pornography, the whores of Satan strutting in their nakedness.

Like this policewoman Rose Shepherd, her head uncovered, her skirts revealing bare ankles and feet. He wished that he had slapped her harder.

He held the Israeli submachine gun, waiting. . . .

The dead men out of his way, David Holden let out the clutch and engaged the throttle, his other hand cutting the wheel, bringing the launch about hard to starboard, toward the yacht, an M-16 leaned beside him, ready.

The gun battle raged on but had shifted way aft, concentrated near the cockpit.

There was no sign of Rosie.

He let the throttle full out.

CHAPTER 5

Rose Shepherd's hand tightened on the UZI carbine pistol-grip and fore end.

She guessed these were the machinery spaces. She could smell oil and diesel fuel and there were massive engines set in against the bulkheads, lines leading into them from farther forward where she had passed fuel storage tanks. Her khaki skirt and robin's-egg-blue blouse were smudged and dirty, her sweater long since tied across her shoulders, and she was still too hot. There were no cool breezes here. The heat from the engines combined with the petroleum smells made the area stifling, sickening. She didn't envy the men who worked here.

She kept moving toward a watertight door ahead of her, half ajar.

As she reached for it, the door swung open and she jumped back. One of the five men in Coast Guard uniforms stabbed a submachine gun toward her. She fired the UZI carbine three times fast, with no time to raise it to proper height. All three hits went to his crotch. His legs swept out from under him as he jackknifed forward and fell across her gun, wrenching the pistol grip from her right hand. Her left arm, entwined in the sling, was almost wrenched out of the shoulder socket. She sucked in her breath with a scream as she stumbled and fell.

As she turned her head, the man with the horrible black eyes was standing over her, a knife at her neck. "Unclean thing," he hissed, moving the knife closer to her throat.

Rose Shepherd balled her right fist and laced him across the tip of the jaw as she squirmed back across the oily floor, trying to extricate the UZI carbine from the dead body lying over it.

The best she could do was free her forearm from the sling.

The man with the evil eyes fell back, left hand touching at his jaw, the knife shaking in his trembling right fist.

He shouted something at her that she couldn't understand.

He came at her with the knife.

"All right, you raghead motherfucker, let's see you strut your stuff," Rose snarled. She jumped to her feet, edging back and whipping off her sweater. She was grateful it was a heavy knit, and wished it were a leather jacket as she balled it around her left forearm, readying herself for his thrust.

She edged farther back, making him come for her, noticing one other man in the now fully open doorway, a leering smile on his street-punk face.

There was a wrench near the portside engine and she grabbed for it. The man with the terrible eyes lunged with his blade, slicing air with a whistling sound, missing her right wrist by inches or less as her fingers closed over the handle of the pipe wrench and snatched it clear.

"Feelin' a little less cocky, asshole?" Rose snapped,

trying to sound brave, even though she was scared to death. His knife—possibly some kind of bayonet—had a blade that looked a foot long.

Scary Eyes moved the knife in his hand, the knife like some living thing under the spell of his eyes, too frightened to do anything but obey and slice through space at his command.

"Come on, slick. Best you can do is some tricks?" She laughed at him, made herself laugh at him.

It was that or scream and cry, and neither one of those would help.

CHAPTER 6

David Holden brought the M-16 into a hard assault position and ran along the yacht's port side with the two crewman who had been waiting by the ladder. There was a heavy concentration of gunfire by the aft companionway.

As he neared the companionway, he could see Dimitropoulous and Captain Selonikas and six other men, gunfire tearing into the coaming. They were in cover on either side of the opening leading below. As Holden joined them, one of Selonikas's crewmen stabbed his UZI into the companionway, firing, but lost the weapon as bullets tore into his left forearm and he fell back, blood spurting from several wounds. Holden clambered over the hatch and grabbed the man, pulling him forward and away from the opening. "We need to stop the bleeding right away or he's gone," Holden shouted. Captain Selonikas was beside Holden and the injured man in the next instant, with a pocket knife cutting away strips of the man's right shirtsleeve while Holden removed the man's belt. Another seaman joined them. "Know how to make a tourniquet?"

"Yes, Professor."

"Then make one. Not too tight." Holden handed the man the belt. More gunfire came from below. "This is useless!" Holden shouted. "How many of them are down there? And where's Rosie?"

"There are five, I think, Rosie! My God! I forgot about Rosie. She was amidships and took shelter in the companionway steps. My God!"

David Holden was up and moving. Dimitropoulous himself and the same two men who'd been by the ladder ran after Holden as he looked back.

"This is where I last saw her!" Dimitropoulous shouted. Holden, the M-16 in his right fist, started below. . . .

If she kept him angry, he wouldn't use the gun. She told herself that as the man with the scary black eyes lunged for her. One of the UZI magazines was in her left hand now, the pipe wrench still in her right.

As his blade crossed toward her, it skittered down the length of the pipe wrench, nearly severing her fingers. But she drew back in time.

She was beside the fuel tanks now, and as she dodged for position, she saw the other man advancing, not with a weapon, but with plastic bags instead, and as he opened the first of them, she saw the tail from a rope of plastic explosive. He started laying it out across the fuel line leading to the starboard engine. "You'll kill yourselves too!"

The man with the evil eyes laughed. "You will be dead before then, whore of Satan!" And he dived toward her. Rosie clubbed at him with the UZI magazine. His blade whipped right. Rosie's right arm drew back and started to swing the pipe wrench. But he moved, his shoulder impacting her by the left temple. He wasn't very tall, but he was stocky, powerfully built. She slipped, fell backward, lost the UZI magazine, the pipe wrench clattering against a fuel tank. As she started to react, his left foot snaked out toward her, impacting her right forearm so hard that after an instant of pain, she had no feeling at all, and the pipe wrench fell from her hand.

She wriggled back across the oily floor, grabbing for the partially empty UZI magazine at the small of her back, the fingers of her left hand closing over it.

As he lunged toward her, she rolled right, her back impacting the fuel tank, then her elbow, causing more pain. Her left arm arced upward between his legs, stabbing the magazine into his testicles.

He actually screamed.

But then he threw himself over her, the knife stabbing downward toward her chest. Her right arm too numb to move, she lost the UZI magazine. She raked her left elbow across his jaw as her right knee smashed up and she spat into his eyes. His knife caught her across the palm of her left hand, but she wouldn't scream.

Somehow she was standing. Her right foot kicked into his neck and she stumbled back.

Hands were on her shoulders.

It was the man with the plastique, his hands like vises, squeezing her downward and together, crushing her. She stomped her left foot back over the arch of his foot and his grip loosened a little. She snapped her left elbow back, missing, his grip tightening again as the one with the scary eyes rose from the floor and started toward her with the knife.

Rose snaked her left hand back, found the man's crotch, and dug her fingers in.

"Bitch!"

But the grip on her shoulders loosed and she pushed herself away from him.

She was between them now, the man who'd been roping out the plastique holding himself as he advanced, the one with the scary eyes making the knife do tricks again.

Her head turned right and left. She edged back. She licked her lips.

The one with the knife dived toward her and she threw herself toward the other one, head-butting him in the abdomen. He fell back. She fell to her knees as the back of his left hand slapped upward across her face.

She sagged back.

Scary Eyes laughed.

"Try *me*!"

It was David's voice.

Scary Eyes wheeled and she saw a blur as a rifle butt snaked outward and upward and Scary Eyes stumbled to his knees.

The one with the explosives was moving his submachine gun on line. Rose saw her pipe wrench on the floor, picked it up in her bleeding left hand, and threw it at his knees. He stumbled, the submachine gun firing into the overhead.

Her ears rang with gunfire as the man's body, rocking with the hits, skidded across the starboard engine and to the deck.

She looked toward David. Behind David, Dimitropoulous and two of Selonikas's sailors held UZI submachine guns and carbines, the muzzles still smoking.

David took a step closer to Scary Eyes.

As Scary Eyes raised his knife, David's right hand moved. He was holding his own knife, and as he thrust it into Scary Eyes's throat and stepped back, Rose Shepherd turned her face away from the blood spray.

CHAPTER 7

It was a small cut, but Holden imagined it hurt like hell as he applied the antiseptic. She was just out of the shower and the wet bandage needed changing. "How's your arm?"

"Sore. But it's okay. You saved my bacon back there." And she leaned toward him and planted a kiss on his cheek.

"That's all I get for saving your life?" Holden joked.

"No—but all you can get right now. Okay?"

"No—but there isn't much choice." He kissed her on the forehead as he finished the bandage to her hand. She stood up, pulling her robe more tightly around her, hair still wet. "You get dressed quick. Now that we're on plan B, so to speak, we're going to be running low on time."

"Gotcha," she sang back over her shoulder, already digging through her suitcase.

Holden went into the bathroom, stripped to his underpants, which were still a little damp from the swim, figured the hell with it, and skinned out of the underpants as well. He started to shave. Plan B, as he'd euphemistically called it, was Tom Ashbrooke's alternate method for Holden and Rosie to reenter the United States.

Through Dimitropoulous, apparently once a

35

world-class smuggler who was a very rich and a very old friend of Tom Ashbrooke's, they had access to any number of vessels that regularly crisscrossed the high seas. The yacht's cover had to be considered blown, so the pickup that was to have been made a few miles offshore was now canceled. Instead, the yacht would rendezvous with a freighter, of the inevitable Liberian registry, and the freighter would bring them to port. The freighter carried automobiles and Holden and Rosie would be smuggled onto the docks inside two of these, the cars to be picked up by an import car company that was owned by Patriots.

He hoped.

Finished shaving, Holden rinsed his razor and put it on the washbasin, then stepped into the shower. . . .

Under other circumstances the setting would have been charming, even romantic. Not that Linda Effingham's company didn't lend itself toward the latter.

Holding hands, they had walked along the beach for nearly an hour, almost back to their point of origin, the hotel where Geoffrey Kearney had first met her. They stopped to watch the water, and the gulls and other seabirds as they dive-bombed the surface, skimmed over it, and went airborne again. Birds weren't the only things flying near the beach. As Kearney began wiggling his bare toes in the sand, he continued his tally of C-130's.

There had been nineteen of them since he'd stopped to remove his shoes when they'd reached the surf, all of them camouflage painted, flying low, coming in for landings at the air base several miles inland. "You must like planes," she said, nuzzling her cheek to his left shoulder.

"I—I do. We don't see that much military traffic in England, at least not over London. When I was a little boy, I used to build airplane models all the time," he lied. He'd always been ten-thumbed at that sort of thing.

"We could go up to my room, Bart."

Geoffrey Kearney looked down at her, still holding her right hand but moving her arm back so he could settle his hand on her waist and still hold her hand in his. "Yes, we could, couldn't we? You know, the last thing I ever expected when I came here for my meeting was that. I'd be finding a way of staying on in the States longer and longer because of a pretty girl."

"Am I just a pretty girl?" She laughed.

Linda Effingham was far more than a pretty girl. Her pansy-blue eyes were set off by long lashes (genuine) in a face just barely starting to lose its summer tan. Her cheekbones were high, like a model's, and her mouth was perfect, lips full, just right. He leaned down and touched his mouth to hers.

She smiled, shook her head, tossing her almost black dark-brown curls.

Along with her physical attributes, such as her fantastic, slightly understated, almost willowy figure, her soft alto voice, and hands that drove him mad with desire, she was an intelligent woman, a good conversationalist, well read, almost erudite—an odd but pleasurable contrast with her slavishness to him in bed.

More important than all of this, she was his wonderfully high-profile reason for staying on at Siamese

Shoals. Printed on the hotel's matchbooks and on everything but the toilet paper was the "Legend of Siamese Shoals." When the hotel was being built in the late nineteenth century near the shoals of the creek on the heights overlooking the ocean, the family building it had been at a loss for an appropriate name. Should it have something to do with the creek, with the shoals, with the promontory above the ocean which the hotel would dominate, or with the beach? There had been a Siamese cat that became a pet to the workmen, and when the owner's young daughter came to the construction site and saw the cat, she began calling the place Siamese Shoals.

The name sounded so natural, it was given to the hotel.

During the Depression years it fell into disrepair. During the war it was partially restored to house officers in pilot training at the air base. After the war the grandson of that little girl bought the place back and restored it to its Victorian luxury. Now it was owned by one of the hotel conglomerates. There was a painting of a little girl with blond ringlets and starched white dress with a Siamese cat on her lap, on the wall over the registration desks. It was supposedly the very child (and the very cat) who had jointly inspired the hotel's name.

It made for a nice story, at any event.

Siamese Shoals was very near to the town of Harrington, North Carolina. And Harrington, North Carolina, from everything Kearney had been able to learn since leaving the safe house near Chicago, was some sort of central receiving area for the Front for the Liberation of North America.

Supposedly the Dumbrowski brothers were still on his trail. He'd left them a wide enough one to keep them away from Carlysle and his wife and Dr. Helen Fletcher and Roy Dumbrowski's wife. But they'd be on the trail of Doctor Phillip Ridgely, the psychiatrist/arsonist, not Bart Kittredge, art dealer on business in the States searching for new and exciting works for his London Galleries.

Eventually, whether in the course of their tracking him (hopefully the Dumbrowski brothers had that much ability) or in some other manner, he'd make contact with them and touch them in a very special way so they would never bother anyone again.

By using their names he'd been able to find his way to Harrington. In likely places throughout northern Illinois and northern Indiana, he'd told the story of how some lunatic had burned down this private psychiatric hospital and how his orders (he'd used various off-the-cuff aliases and accents) had been to report there. But how could he report to a place which no longer existed?

In time, through his search, Harrington, North Carolina, began to surface as the successor to the now defunct Cedar Ridge Islands resort, closed and occupied by the United States Marshals Service, fewer than seventy-five miles from Siamese Shoals.

Holden wondered if Siamese Shoals might somehow be connected to Cedar Ridge Islands and the FLNA, but all of the guests seemed perfectly normal; they were not Middle Eastern and Central European types wearing American clothes awkwardly and smiling instead of talking because they didn't want to reveal a killing accent.

The people at Siamese Shoals seemed like well-off tourists and vacationers, happy to get away to the Old World amenities and escape the reality of the broadening war in the United States with the FLNA and the frightening, inexorable deterioration of their own government now under the control of de facto President Roman Makowski. The real President still lay in a coma; official word in newspapers and broadcast television seemed to be preparing the American people for the inevitable and seemed to vie for attention with the routine litanies of terror atrocities, more and more of which were being laid at the feet of the Patriots rather than the FLNA.

The new laws concerning firearms were the only thing that seemed to dominate the news more than the President or the terror.

According to Executive Order 128946 it was unlawful to possess most types of firearms, and federalized National Guard units were raiding, without warrant, homes of persons suspected of keeping such firearms secretly.

At the present rate, with the suspension of habeas corpus and of provisions against unlawful search and seizure, these Americans might indeed wish they'd never parted with the Mother Country.

The thought amused Geoffrey Kearney, but not terribly much.

"Well?"

He looked down at Linda Effingham. "Lunch?"

"Food or me?"

"How about you first, then food?"

"But we'll eat downstairs. I brought all these pretty dresses and all I ever seem to do is stay in them for five minutes and then you're unzipping me."

"Can I help it that I'm only human darling?" He touched his lips to her forehead.

Linda Effingham was many things indeed.

It would be hard to leave her. She was more than physically marvelous. Kearney thought he really loved her. But somewhere in Harrington, North Carolina, there was an answer, an answer to the very important question of the whereabouts of the mysterious Dimitri Borsoi.

And Kearney had to find Dimitri Borsoi, learn all that he could about how to destroy the FLNA, and then kill him.

That was, after all, what the British Secret Intelligence Service had sent him to the United States to do in the first place. And with each day that passed, his passion for destroying the Front for the Liberation of North America and Borsoi and all the rest rooted more deeply in him than the passion for any woman.

Kearney held Linda Effingham a little more tightly as they walked away from the surf, toward the rocks and the two hundred forty-three stairs that led upward from the beach to Siamese Shoals.

There wouldn't be that much more time left to hold her.

CHAPTER 8

Rose Shepherd had always wanted to ride in a Rolls-Royce, but never in the trunk.

It was roomy enough, and with the oxygen bottle she could breathe comfortably.

She shifted position, her legs cramping a little. She felt for the Walther P-5 and extra magazines in the darkness, then just for the heck of it twisted on the single-cell Maglite she'd taken out of her purse and slipped into the pocket of her blue jeans.

They were traveling light, each of them with a single bag. After getting David out of Peru and to the safe house the Israelis had set up for them to use in Fortaleza, she'd been very much tempted to hit some of the shops. But she hadn't, because she'd known that almost anything she bought would likely get left behind and, anyway, what good was a pink linen sundress when you spent all of your time wearing battle dress utilities, carrying guns, and fighting the FLNA?

She'd bought the pink linen sundress anyway, but only that. It was rolled, wrapped in plastic, and in the bottom of the bag that she was sharing Rolls-Royce trunk space with now.

At least she could try it on for David. There hadn't been time for that and she hadn't thought about it after the first night on Dimitropoulous's yacht. She'd taken it out, hung it up in the hope of letting the wrinkles fall out, and David had taken her to bed and she forgot about the sundress. There had been a lot of bed aboard the yacht, some walks around the deck, some talks with Dimitropoulous about the network Tom Ashbooke was setting up to smuggle in medical supplies and ammunition and arms for the Patriots. And more bed.

She hugged her arms to herself.

Soon she'd be out of the trunk and into David's arms. And back to the war. . . .

David Holden watched as the silver-gray Rolls was lifted on the crane, swayed slightly—at least Rosie usually had a strong stomach—and started out over the deck.

His car was a Bentley. He'd deferred to Rosie, since she'd always wanted to ride in a Rolls-Royce.

The captain of the Liberian-registry freighter, a black man of about forty-five with a thin mustache and a Jamaican accent, said, "I wish we had been given the opportunity to talk, Doctor Holden. I was a serious student of history in my schooldays and I understand you are quite the authority."

"The news-magazine articles, right?" Holden smiled, catching up his black ballistic nylon bag.

"You are a very famous man."

"Some might say infamous, Captain Downey. But perhaps we'll meet again." Holden tossed the bag into the open trunk of the Bentley, checked the Desert Eagle in its side pouch, then started to step in.

"I hope that we do meet again, Doctor Holden." Captain Downey extended his hand and David Holden took it, the captain's handclasp firm and dry. "Have a pleasant ride. I always somehow preferred a Bentley over a Rolls-Royce anyway."

"I'll remember that." Holden nodded, stepping inside completely now, trying to figure out what to do with his legs besides breaking them off. He was sitting on the Walther P-5 that was in his hip pocket. He moved that.

"Are you secure, sir?"

"Yes, Captain, thank you." He ducked his head as the freighter captain started lowering the trunk lid.

It slammed shut. There was a tap on the lid, a muffled voice, and Holden suddenly felt very claustrophobic. With the Mini Maglite from his shirt pocket he found the oxygen bottle again and checked it one more time. He pulled the mask over his head and secured it over his mouth and nose.

He turned off the flashlight.

There was a sensation of motion.

He pictured what was happening from what he had observed with Rosie and the Rolls-Royce.

The car was rising slowly, swaying—he could feel that well enough in the pit of his stomach—and the swaying seemed to ease as there was a lurch.

He could definitely feel directional movement.

Holden closed his eyes. Rosie would be on the dock by now. Soon he'd be joining her. . . .

Rose Shepherd banged her head on something and all motion stopped. She inhaled slowly, waiting for someone to open the trunk lid. It should be someone she knew, someone from the Metro Patriot cell, sent to meet them at the original drop-off point, then alerted to the change—at least if everything had gone as scheduled.

Maybe Patsy Alfredi, or Mitch Diamond. Whoever it was, she longed for a friendly face after all this darkness.

The trunk lid didn't open.

Her right hand was on the butt of the Walther P-5. It was a great little gun, but she'd feel happier with her own guns.

The trunk lid still wasn't opened.

It wasn't as if she could start banging on it or something, because it had to be opened by the right person. If a security policeman opened it and saw her inside . . .

She took the bead-ended rubber band out of her ponytail and redid it, but there was no room to be able to properly brush her hair.

The trunk lid was still closed and her breathing was getting harder, faster. There was enough oxygen in the bottle for forty-five minutes. They'd told her that. She pushed the little button on her Ironman—she wore both watches and that was the fashion anyway—and read the time. She had been inside the trunk of the Rolls-Royce for twelve minutes. Thirty-three minutes remained on the oxygen bottle.

No problem.

The trunk lid would probably open up in a few minutes, and anyway, there was enough oxygen without the bottle. A little stuffy, but she wouldn't smother. She could stay inside the trunk for hours.

She licked her lips. It was like being locked inside

an expensive coffin. What if she had to urinate? What if—

Rose Shepherd realized she was frightened and it was stupid to be frightened but she was frightened anyway.

CHAPTER 9

Dimitri Borsoi was very disappointed in the way ibn-
Mu'adh had performed aboard the yacht. It was impossible to know just exactly what had gone wrong, of
course, or even if ibn-Mu'adh was alive or dead, but
the fact remained that David Holden and Rose Shepherd were reported aboard the *Princess Maria*. That
they were alive was enough.

He had considered the options carefully when
working out a fallback scenario.

If the attempt to kill them failed, Dimitropoulous
would likely feel that trying to go through with the rest
of the initial plan was frought with peril. Much better
to initiate the alternate plan. There was no way Dimitropoulous could know that the International Islamic
Jihad owned various persons at the Monrovia, Liberia,
docks and, through one of these, controlled the chief
engineer aboard the *Princess Maria*.

And International Islamic Jihad owed favors to
Dimitri Borsoi that could never be repaid.

Immediately, when he learned that the *Princess
Maria* was the backup means for Holden and Shepherd
to reenter the United States, he set about learning all
that he could about the vessel and its cargo.

Automobiles were the perfect thing. Large rich-
persons' automobiles with large trunks in which an
adult, male or female, could easily be hidden.

It was well known that the rank and file of the unions for the dockworkers, despite what their leadership might say to the contrary, were solidly pro Patriot.

It would be a simple matter to get Holden and Shepherd out of the trunk or trunks and spirited to safety.

So they thought.

This time, it would work.

CHAPTER 10

David Holden, his flashlight in his teeth, was working to dismantle the lock on the Bentley's trunk lid. Something had gone wrong. The dockworkers, like most of rank-and-file organized labor, supported the Patriots, in some cases very actively. Often union truckers would alert the Patriots to suspicious shipments that might be arms or explosives destined for the FLNA. Union pilots would spot suspicious sites from the air, sites that might be FLNA strongholds, and alert Patriot cells. Because of the dockworkers the Patriot cell in San Francisco had scored a substantial victory over the FLNA, capturing a small but very precious cargo of electronic detonators that would have been used to trigger FLNA bombs across the country. But something was wrong here. If the Patriot members who had been assigned to meet Rosie and himself hadn't been reached in time to guarantee assistance, there was a backup system of several trusted dockworkers, themselves Patriots, who had been already lined up to free Rosie and Holden from the car trunks.

But where were they?

Holden kept working at dismantling the lock. Bentleys were built tough. So was his Leatherman tool. But the Leatherman tool, he at last resigned himself, just wasn't adequate to the task. A pry bar might do the trick.

With the flashlight still in his teeth, its vague metallic taste on his tongue, he attacked the problem from a different perspective.

He could go out through the rear seat into the car itself. But that method would be time consuming in the extreme. David Holden began searching on the Bentley's trunk for a jack handle. If Bentleys were shipped with the jacks already installed. . . .

The trunk lid opened.

Rose Shepherd squinted against the light.

The faces, hard to distinguish in the glare, weren't familiar looking.

"Hello?" She had her borrowed pistol ready.

"We came to get you, Detective Shepherd," said a voice belonging to one of the faces.

She kept squinting, trying to see more clearly. They were young faces, perhaps a little too young?

Rose shepherd turned her face away from the sun so she could see a little more clearly.

Both men were holding guns and there were three more men and a woman behind them. "What's going on, guys?"

"Reception committee," one of them said with a laugh. And then Rose Shepherd realized that the guns the young men held were pointed at her. . . .

David Holden averted his eyes and pressed down on the pry-barlike jack handle with all the leverage and strength he could muster within the confined space of the trunk. There was a popping sound and something metallic impacted his right forearm. It stung a bit, but he didn't think he was wounded.

He reached for the .44 Magnum Desert Eagle in the side pouch of his opened bag.

As he raised the trunk lid, the Desert Eagle in his right fist, the safety off and the hammer under his thumb, he squinted against the low sun's brightness.

To his left was the edge of the dock. To his right he saw six people, four men and two women, all in rough work clothes. One of the men was drawing a gun, two others already held guns, and one of the women was trying to open the trunk of another Bentley.

Holden started out of the Bentley trunk, watching them. One of the men gestured with the muzzle of his gun toward the front of the other car. Another of the six ran around, seemed to study the windshield—there were numbers soaped onto it—and shouted, "Wrong damn car, Les!"

Holden was fully out of the Bentley now, the fresh air making him a little lightheaded. There had been several Bentleys aboard the *Princess Maria,* waiting to be off-loaded onto the docks. But only one Rolls-Royce.

Holden shivered. "Rosie."

Everything in the bag he had was expendable except for his knife and the shoulder holster for his Beretta, taken off the dead body of Innocentio Hernandez. He pulled out the shoulder rig with two extension magazines and empty holster. He removed the knife and sheath from it, slid the knife into his belt, and stuffed the holster inside his shirtfront. Three spare magazines for the Desert Eagle—he hadn't expected a shooting war—went into his pockets. He dropped the bag, now useless to him, into the trunk.

Holden backed away, the six beside the other Bentley starting to turn around and look his way.

They could be Patriot dockworkers.

But somehow there was something wrong about them.

Holden heard a shot from farther up the docks. He wheeled toward the sound. *Rosie*.

"Hey!"

Holden looked toward the six.

Another of them shouted, "It's him! Get him, dammit!"

A pistol-sized submachine gun was pointed toward him. David Holden threw himself down beside the Bentley, bullets tearing into the still-open trunk lid and the left rear fender, pinging off the metal, ripping jagged holes through it.

David Holden was up and moving. He reached the hood of the Bentley. The one with the pistol-sized submachine gun was putting a fresh magazine up the well. As the other five set themselves to open fire, Holden fired first, the Desert Eagle rocking in his right fist, sending the submachine gunner's body stumbling back, spinning around and falling to the dock.

Holden ran. The Bentley's windshield shattered behind him.

"Rosie!"

More gunfire came from ahead of him.

He rounded a stacked row of packing crates. He could see three men and a woman crouched at the rear of the Rolls-Royce, its trunk lid open. "Rosie!" Another man was on the dock surface, his body twisted at an unnatural angle. Still another lay half in, half out of the trunk itself.

"David!"

It was Rosie's voice, from farther up the docks, near more of the packing crates.

Holden fired the Desert Eagle as one of the four from beside the Rolls-Royce turned toward him and fired. A bullet whistled past Holden's left ear. The man who'd shot at Holden went down, clutching his chest.

Holden veered right, looking back over his shoulder. The five from the short gunfight beside the Bentley were after him.

Three more were by the Rolls.

He kept running. Rosie stepped out from behind cover, her pistol in her hands. "Drop, David!"

Holden dropped and heard gunfire from behind him. He rolled. Gunfire came from Rosie's direction. A man was down. Holden stabbed the Desert Eagle toward their pursuers, firing, then firing again. Another one of them was shot down.

He was up on his feet, shouting to Rosie, "Run for it!"

She fired past him, then turned, breaking into a dead run. Holden was almost even with her now.

He looked back.

There were six of them, still, but one of them held his left arm stiffly at his side.

"David! It was a trap!"

"Keep running." Holden slowed, turned around, fired a double tap with the Desert Eagle, taking down one of the two women.

He fired the last two rounds indiscriminately, to slow up the pursuit, then he was running again. Rosie, crouched beside the gangplank of a freighter, shouted, "Dodge to your right, David!"

Holden dodged right, as gunfire tore into a row of packing crates. Rosie's pistol fired a double tap, then another. Holden pocketed the empty magazine for the Desert Eagle, finished the tactical change, rammed the fresh magazine up the butt of his gun as his right thumb pressured down the slide release.

He stabbed the pistol behind him, firing two shots fast.

The wounded man was down dead. One of the two remaining women was doubled up in a ball beside some of the packing crates, rolling on the dock surface, clutching her left thigh.

From the other end of the docks, behind Rosie, Holden saw a van speeding toward them. "Look out!"

The door on the side of the van opened; submachine-gun fire laced a furrow along the dock surface. Holden raised the Desert Eagle in both fists, fired, then fired again, shattering the windshield of the van. The van swerved, crashing into an eight-foot-high stack of what looked like cotton bales, and a man's body flew through one of the windshield panels, bounced onto the dock surface, skidded, stopped.

"Up the gangplank, Rosie! Hurry!"

Holden backed toward it, firing two more rounds from the Desert Eagle, nailing another of their original pursuers. He looked toward the crashed van. Two men were stumbling out of it, one of them with a submachine gun, the other with an assault rifle. Holden fired, emptying the Desert Eagle, putting the submachine gunner down.

Holden turned up the gangplank and ran. Rosie was firing her P-5 from the height of it. "I'm out, David!"

Holden rammed a fresh magazine up the well of the Desert Eagle. This one and one more spare, only sixteen rounds, were all he had.

He reached the height of the gangplank. The vessel was a tanker of some type—not a floating city, like the ocean-going supertankers, but it was at least two or three blocks long, by far the largest vessel at the docks. "I'm really out. No more ammo. Nothing."

Holden grabbed Rosie's hand, shifted the Desert Eagle to his left, and ran with her. A man appeared from a hatchway. Holden turned the muzzle of the Desert Eagle toward him, and the man's hands went up as he drew back. Holden let him go and ran toward the seaward side of the tanker. From behind them he heard gunfire. Bullets ripped into the metal decking just ahead of them sending a shower of sparks in their wake with the pinging of ricochets.

Holden let go of Rosie's hand, turned, and dropped to his knees beside an open tank hatch, shouting, "Keep going!"

There was no time to look to see if she complied, although he doubted she would. The Desert Eagle was up in both fists. Holden fired, the first shot a miss, the second shot good. The man from the van who had the assault rifle slammed back and down. The remaining woman and one of the men charged toward Holden screaming obscenities. Holden fired, then fired again, shooting the man down. The other man, who had stayed back, had the assault rifle now, and was spraying it toward Holden. Holden fell back as the deck less than three feet in front of him took the hits, a shower of sparks, bits and pieces of lead, and gilding metal and steel from the deck plates raining around him. He closed his eyes against the debris.

He heard Rosie's voice over the ringing in his ears. "David!"

Holden opened his eyes. The woman standing over him, bringing the muzzle of her pistol down toward his chest, hissed "Kiss your—"

"You kiss yours, honey!" It was Rosie's voice. Rosie's right foot snaked out, impacting the woman in the right rib-cage, sending her sprawling. Her pistol fired, tearing into the tank hatch beside him, ricocheting.

Holden was up. The remaining man charged toward them, firing his assault rifle. Holden punched the Desert Eagle toward the man and fired, then again and again. All three shots connected, the assault rifle spraying out across the deck plates. The body was sent twisting and fell.

Holden looked to his left. Rosie Shepherd's left hand was locked to the woman's gun-hand wrist, the pistol discharging into the air. Rosie took a half step back. Her tiny right fist straight-armed into the woman's windpipe, then Rosie's right arm snapped back and rammed forward again, palm bent up and back, the heel of Rosie's hand impacting the base of the woman's nose.

The gun fell from dead fingers.

Rosie stumbled forward to one knee, then stood

up, the dead woman's pistol—a Beretta or a Taurus, Holden couldn't be sure at the distance—in Rosie's right hand. "Half a magazine."

"This time you saved my bacon."

Rosie Shepherd smiled. "Let's get the hell out of here and then we discuss repaying each other, huh?"

Holden grabbed Rosie by the hand and they ran.

CHAPTER 11

There hadn't been any lunch.

Geoffrey Kearney stepped out of the shower and toweled himself dry, dressing quickly in his light gray slacks and a light blue dress shirt.

As he threaded his belt into the trouser loops, his feet still bare, he walked toward his window. The sun was setting. If he kept spending all his time making love with Linda Effingham, he'd never get anything done.

But, Kearney consoled himself, it was great fun and he was, after all, cementing his cover as an idle vacationer. Try explaining that one to headquarters, he thought, smiling. He lit a cigarette as he searched for a pair of gray socks, found them, and started pulling them on.

The thing that most unnerved him was working deep inside enemy territory without weapons. He was accustomed to that sort of thing in the Eastern Bloc countries (although he never really got used to it), but in a Western nation, as long as one avoided what appeared to be overt criminal acts, one should feel reasonably safe from unprovoked police searches.

This was no longer the case in the States.

To have taken one of his weapons from the special compartments in the Ford he was driving would have been risking either incarceration or a shootout with the police, neither of which was what he'd come to this country for.

He whipped his necktie under his collar and knotted it quickly, closing the collar button as he walked toward the closet, stuffing his feet into his shoes.

He pulled up the knit tie from half-mast and took his blue blazer off the hanger in the closet.

He crossed the room to the nightstand, catching up his wallet with his fake driver's license, fake credit cards, and the like. He slipped his fake passport into the breast pocket of the jacket.

At least the money in his clip was real.

"Handkerchief," he said aloud, walking back to the dresser and taking one, pocketing it along with keys to the car, cigarettes and lighter, and his room key.

He exited the room and walked along the open porch, looking down on the shoals of the creek—in his country it would have qualified as a small river—taking a last drag on his cigarette.

As he stopped before Linda Effingham's door, he stubbed out the cigarette in a small ashtray set out from the wall.

He had a key to her room, but he knocked anyway.

The door opened almost under his hand.

She was beautiful.

But that in itself was nothing remarkable, because she was always beautiful. Her almost black hair was up and she wore a white sundress that showed off her expensive tan. "I'm all ready." She smiled, leaning up to kiss him on the mouth. He kissed her back, but not too hard. If they started that again, he'd miss dinner too. "Just have to get my shawl and my purse."

"Our reservations aren't for another fifteen minutes anyway. We can have a drink at the bar, if you'd like."

"Sounds good." She reappeared in the doorway, a small evening bag in her hand and a knitted shawl over her arm. "All set."

As she passed by him, he could smell her perfume again.

"Easy," he whispered to himself, pulling her door closed behind him. . . .

The Siamese Shoals hotel bar was elegant yet understated, its paneling better than Kearney had ever seen in a minister's office or a corporate boardroom, the lighting subdued but not to the point where trying to look at something brought on a headache.

There was a very large, expensive-looking television set at each end of the bar, tuned to a cable sports station. Reruns of the last Olympic Winter Games were playing. Kearney's eyes focused from time to time on the giant slalom skiers, then would shift back to Linda Effingham.

In her lovely, naturally ladylike way, Linda Effingham sipped occasionally at a gin-and-tonic Kearney'd ordered for her. Kearney, ableit a bit more robustly, sipped occasionally at his glass of Cutty Sark.

The man sitting at the bar two stools away didn't sip at his Jack Daniel's Black Label. He gulped. And the fellow might well get himself arrested for something or other if he kept talking the way he was,

Kearney thought absently. Free speech hadn't officially been banned by one of Roman Makowski's ever-proliferating executive orders, but Kearney had no doubt that something to the same effect was already sitting on Makowski's expropriated presidential desk, awaiting just the right moment to be promulgated. ". . . sucks the way these days they seem to be takin' the Constitution apart a line at a time. That Roman Makowski. Wish someone'd blown him up instead of the real President."

Kearney lit the rare cigarette for Linda Effingham, his thoughts elsewhere as he pocketed the Zippo. The man at the bar, certainly a little drunk, and more than a little talkative, was making telling points. There were likely a great many people who would have much preferred Roman Makowski to be expected never to come out of a coma rather than the President the American people had elected, and doubtless would have elected forever if the law had permitted.

The bartender, a very proper-looking black man with a rich baritone voice, leaned toward the talking man and whispered something Kearney couldn't hear and didn't bother straining to listen to.

But Kearney could hear the talking man's response. Anyone in the bar, or, for that matter, in the lobby of Siamese Shoals, could have heard it. "Let Roman Makowski come on down here and talk to people. They'll tell him what an asshole he is."

Abruptly the man stopped, turned toward Kearney and Linda Effingham, and smiled, "Forgive me, sir; I hope I didn't offend your lady, there."

Kearney looked at Linda. "Were you offended, darling?"

She licked her pretty lips and looked down into her drink.

Kearney looked back at the talking man. "I think she'll survive; but you might be better off, old man, watching your choice of words a bit closer." It was as much a rebuke as Kearney could risk without also risking a fight. And a fight with a drunk was all he needed, even a generally pleasant drunk like this fellow.

The talking man smiled. "You're a true gentleman, sir."

"Thank you." Kearney nodded.

"Aren't American, either, are you?"

Kearney nodded and smiled. "I'm what you'd call a Brit. But we British are keenly aware of the problems you chaps are having in the States these days and are truly sorry for them."

"Well, hell, the English have been our allies in all the world wars. You'd kinda know they'd be worryin' about us. I wish your queen or somebody'd tell Makowski to take a hike. Maybe he'd listen to her. He sure doesn't listen to the American people."

"Well, I'm sure the queen wouldn't really be the person to do that. Actually, our royalty is more ceremonial than political. Or at least it's supposed to be that way."

"Well, then, your prime minister."

"The PM hasn't consulted me on the issue lately." Kearney smiled, lighting a cigarette for himself.

The talking man laughed as he half stood and slid

down the two stools necessary to bring him to Kearney's right side. He extended his hand. "I'm Amos Whistler."

Kearney took the fellow's hand—he had a dry, solid handclasp—and introduced himself and the lady beside him. Her face was starting to turn red at the cheeks. "I'm Bartholomew Kittredge. And this is Miss Effingham. A pleasure to meet you, Mr. Whistler."

"Amos. Amos. And it's real nice meeting you, miss. Everybody calls me Amos."

"My friends call me Bart." Geoffrey Kearney felt Linda Effingham's elbow nudge against his rib cage. He looked into his drink and winked at her with his left eye.

"Well, Bart, got any brothers named Bret or Beau?" And Amos Whistler laughed.

"I watch old American western shows too. I'm afraid I'm not even a good poker player," Kearney lied.

Amos Whistler started laughing again. Kearney, in a flash of understanding, realized why so many stand-up comics got their start as lounge acts. Get the right amount of lubrication into some people and they'd laugh at anything.

"Whatcha do if you don't play poker, Bart?"

Kearney smiled in spite of himself. "I'm an art dealer. Here in the States buying up some new things for my galleries."

"Art? Damn! I'm into art. I collect all sorts of stuff. Everything from Cachina dolls to Salvador Dalí and back again. You oughta come see."

Kearney didn't know what to say, so he said nothing at all, usually the best course.

"I live just a coupla miles from here, over past Harrington. Got all the stuff stored in a big old vault. These days, you can't be too careful."

"Well, sometime—"

"Look, Bart"—and Amos Whistler turned around on his stool—"why not now?"

Kearney looked at his drink. "I'd really love to, but the young lady and I have reservations for dinner." Kearney glanced at the Rolex on his left wrist. "Speaking of which—"

Amos Whistler lowered his voice. "Art, like beauty, is in the eye of the beholder. If you're not interested in my paintings and such, maybe you'd like to see the Dumbrowski brothers, Doctor Ridgely, because they're sure interested in seeing you."

Kearney started to turn around. "You can walk out of here right now with me and the girl doesn't get hurt, see? She can just keep right on walking while you go for a little ride. Or you can tough it out and those four folks over at the table in the far corner—go on, take a look at them"—Kearney did just that. Two men and two women sat at the table, the women carrying large purses, the men wearing loose-fitting windbreakers. Both men hoisted their glasses in Kearney's direction—"they'll start shooting at you and sure as God made little green apples, Miss Effingham here will die."

Kearney looked at Linda Effingham, then at Amos Whistler. "You'll die, too, friend. I promise you that. If anything happens to her."

"I'll bet you know that karate shit real good."

"Bart?" Linda hissed from behind him.

"It'll be all right," Kearney told her, reaching out and squeezing her hand.

"Question is, do you want her to die? You and I are in this thing, different sides and everything, but we're in it. She isn't in it at all. So, you go ahead and choose." And he raised his voice. "I'd sure love it if you'd come by my place, just for a little while. You and the lady'd have an experience you'd never forget." There was a smile on Amos Whistler's face that Kearney didn't like at all.

"Well," Kearney said, raising his voice a little, "it does sound like wonderful fun. And I suppose I owe it to my business to take a look. Wouldn't be interested in selling a Dalí, would you? Times are hard, I know, but the market's very strong."

Amos Whistler fell into it nicely. "Well, you may be right. I guess it'd depend on what you offer, Bart."

"Well," Kearney volunteered, "then you wait here, and I'll go cancel our reservations." Kearney was up out of the stool. He bent over and kissed Linda, walking out of the bar as he said, "I'll only be a moment, darling."

He was out of the bar.

He breathed. They'd kill Linda anyway, but at least this way there was a chance to get her out of it alive.

He started for the maître d's podium-style desk, glancing back toward the bar. One of the two men from the corner table exited the bar, stopped by the telephones near the men's room door, and watched him.

A woman was at the podium-style desk. "Hi. My

name's Kittredge. I have a reservation for two. Afraid I have to cancel."

He didn't wait for a reply, but started walking back across the lobby. The man from the corner table was still beside the telephone. Kearney walked toward the men's room door and went inside. What he had to do would have to be done quickly, or else the situation in the bar would deteriorate and Linda would die.

He went into a stall, closed the door, kicked the toilet seat down with his foot, and stood on it, crouching, hearing the door from the lobby opening just as he did. He was in luck; the door hinges were tight enough so that the door stayed partially closed without being locked.

"Hey. Doctor Ridgely, or whatever your name is. Out now or she gets it right here, along with everybody else in the bar."

Kearney didn't move.

He heard the door to the first stall being opened, kicked. Then the second.

He was in the third.

When the third stall door was kicked inward, Kearney kicked it back, as hard and fast as he could, jumping down from the toilet seat and through the doorway, catching the man from the bar on the shoulders with both hands. There was a pistol in the man's right hand. Kearney knee-smashed the man in the groin, then again and again. Kearney's right fist crossed his jaw, then Kearney's right elbow did the same in one fluid motion.

Kearney's left hand was on the gun. He wheeled around left, both hands locked on the pistol and the man's gun-hand wrist. Kearney smashed his left elbow into the man's solar plexus, the heel of his left foot smashing down over the instep of the man's left foot, then mule-kicked into the man's left knee. Kearney's left elbow smashed back again, throwing his body weight back. Kearney slammed the man into the wall.

The grip on the gun loosened and Kearney ripped it free, turning out and away left, a full one hundred eighty degrees, making a double tae kwon do kick to the man's chest and groin.

The man from the bar was unconscious before he fell, his face distorted, nose broken, and vomit pouring from his lips.

Geoffrey Kearney left him where he lay. There was no time for niceties, only time to kill him. Kearney did that with a fast hard blow from the gun butt—the pistol was a Colt Officer's ACP .45—to the man's neck at the base of the skull.

A quick pat-down to the logical places produced two spare magazines and a wallet.

Kearney pocketed these as he went out the men's room door.

A man was starting to enter, Kearney telling him, "There's a chap in terrible shape inside. I wouldn't go in if I were you."

He walked quickly toward the lobby doors, hugging the wall as well as he could so he couldn't be seen from the bar.

The night was cool, to the west, the sky was a beautiful purple.

As soon as he was clear of the door, Kearney broke into a dead run to his right, checking the little Colt's condition of readiness. One round was in the chamber. It was cocked and locked, with six rounds in the magazine.

He reached the bar service door. When he checked in at a hotel, his first order of business, whenever time allowed, was to learn all the entrances and exits. Time had allowed this time and he was glad that it had.

He tried the door.

It didn't open.

"Damn!"

Kearney stepped back, momentarily debating what to do. It was only the secret agents in movies who always had their moves planned out perfectly. He knocked at the door, in his best American accent singing out, "Delivery for the Smith wedding! Hey, Mac!"

Kearney waited. In another sixty seconds or less the dead man in the lavatory would be discovered, and if not sooner, Amos Whistler and his happy band would kill or kidnap Linda Effingham. "Hey!" He hammed on the door with the flat of his left hand, the little Colt .45 automatic behind his right thigh, the safety dropped, the hammer still cocked.

The door opened. "Hey, guy, I got people—"

It was the black bartender. "Get out here," Kearney rasped, pointing the gun at his chest. The man stepped through, Kearney catching the door. "Locks when it closes?"

"Yes, sir, but—"

"The woman I came in with—still at the bar?"

"With that guy who was drinking so much. What—"

"Stay clear and you'll be all right"—he read the man's name off the name tag, adding, "Herb. Here's for the drinks and the service"—and Kearney flipped him a twenty out of the dead man's wallet.

Kearney went inside, pulling the door to, squinting to see, trying to accustom his eyes to the lower light level.

He was in a storage room, nearly as dimly lit as the bar, with only a single bare bulb on a pull-chain-activated cord swinging over the center of the room. Cases of expensive liquor were stacked everywhere and cases of cheaper stuff too. He assumed these were the house brands.

Kearney crossed the room, eyes nearly accustomed to the dim light.

He reached the swinging door at the back of the bar. He tightened his fist on the butt of the gun. It would have to be very quick.

As he stepped through into the area behind the bar, Amos Whistler was standing up, pulling Linda Effingham off her barstool, his right hand in the side pocket of his suit coat.

Kearney stabbed the little pistol toward him, firing it once, the shot hitting Whistler in the right temple. "Linda! Down! On the floor!"

She dropped.

One of the women from the corner booth was pulling a pistol from her big purse. Kearney shot her through the right forearm and into the chest and she flopped back. The second woman had a gun in her hand and fired. A bottle beside Kearney's right shoulder smashed as Kearney squinted against the spray and fired a single shot to her neck.

The man from the table was in motion, running for the door.

Kearney led him for two steps as the man raised his pistol. Kearney shot him twice, once through the left upper arm, hoping to penetrate into the rib cage and lung, the second time in the thorax as the man spun toward him and fired as he was already stumbling back, the bullet shattering a mirror in the ceiling of the bar.

"Seven years bad luck," Kearney murmured under his breath. "Poor chap." Kearney buttoned out the little Colt's nearly emptied magazine, swapping it for a fresh one from his pocket as he jumped up onto the bar, swung his legs around, dropped down, and fell to a crouch beside Linda Effingham.

"Take me with you. Whoever you are," she whispered, her voice so hoarse with emotion it sounded unreal, her whole body trembling.

"Can't very well leave you here, can I?" Kearney smiled. "Stay close." He started across the bar, just now noticing the little screams, the tears, and the horrified whispers of the rest of the patrons of the bar.

He grabbed Linda's right hand in his left, propelling her along. "Come on!"

They were at the doorway into the lobby.

A security guard was running toward them. "Damn," Kearney murmured, and snapped Linda in front of him as if she were a shield, putting his gun beside her head, his finger beside the trigger guard, not inside it. "Look frightened."

"That's—that's—"

"Hold it!" The security guard dropped into an old obsolete FBI combat crouch, his revolver at the ready.

Kearney snapped back to him, "Come at me and the girl's brains are all over your lovely wallpaper. Your choice. Think of the lawsuits. Reckless conduct, all of that."

The security guard rose up slightly, raising the muzzle of his revolver as well.

Kearney edged toward the doorway out of the lobby, eyes shifting right and left, waiting for someone admirably heroic but with poor timing to try to stop him.

No one did, which didn't reinforce his faith in humanity that terribly much.

They were through the lobby doors. "Have to be my car, I'm afraid. Some things in it I'll need," Kearney told her, pulling her back, crossing into the driveway.

"You—you wouldn't have—"

"If you'd thought I were that sort, you wouldn't have asked to come along, would you?" Kearney smiled.

She sagged against him.

The car was a good two hundred yards deep into the parking lot, but, on the plus side, it was parked nose out for a fast getaway.

"Just keep walking backwards, Linda. Although yours are beautiful, of course, it's great exercise for firm calves, actually," Kearney advised.

Things were not going well, on one level, but at least he was in the right place for finding the FLNA and the Dumbrowski brothers. If he could get one of them to talk, that information could be the most solid lead he'd had yet to finding Dimitri Borsoi.

There were complications, of course, such as getting out of the parking lot alive. And there was also Linda Effingham.

The worst part about Linda was that he really did love her.

"Damn."

"What?"

"Nothing. Keep walking, darling."

CHAPTER 12

They were on their third stolen car, bypassing Metro by as wide a margin as they could. The ammoless Walther P-5 sat in the glove compartment. The car, a Ford station wagon just a few years old but running terribly rough, was the fourth vehicle they'd stolen today, their first an expropriated speedboat they'd used to get out of the dock area.

The Desert Eagle was on the seat between them, its solitary fully loaded magazine up the butt, a ninth round in the chamber. The pistol was a dead giveaway should they be stopped by the police for a routine inspection, but not nearly as dead a giveaway as their faces. With the two of them—David Holden and Rosie Shepherd—together, only a blind man or an imbecile would fail to recognize them as wanted. Their pictures were in every post office across the nation, his picture on the cover of news magazines and newspapers, and both their pictures on the evening news at least one or two nights each week.

There was a new television program that had just started, Rosie told him. It was called *Terror Watch*. Each week a prominent Patriot leader from one cell or another across the country was to be profiled, and calls were solicited on an 800 number from anyone who might have seen the man or woman.

David Holden felt less than honored and even less

happy that he, as Rosie had told him, was the subject of the first week's program, "Rogue History Professor."

"Kind of a dumb title," Holden said at last.

"What is?"

"That 'Rogue History Professor' thing."

"Oh, well, that wasn't the actual title. They just kept referring to you that way. You were cute when you were a little boy, that sailor suit and everything."

"Sailor suit?"

"When you were four years old. At your aunt's house."

"Four . . . ? Holy—" He remembered the picture very well, suddenly. His aunt had been rather well off. Not as well off as she'd thought, but better off than most. He'd been sent to spend a few weeks with her over the summer when he was little. He remembered incidents from those days vaguely. But he remembered the pictures very clearly. His aunt, he'd always suspected, was a little on the nutso side. And she wasn't really his aunt, just a close friend of his mother's. She'd always wanted children, never had any of her own, and lavished toys on him and expensive presents until, he'd learned years later, his father had seen the pictures from that summer.

"Thank God it was the one with the sailor suit," Holden said aloud.

"What?"

"Nothing."

"No—what do you mean?" Rosie pressed.

He looked at her across the seat, his mouth suddenly dry. "She wasn't really my aunt, you know? Just a friend of my mom's. She was a little crazy, maybe.

My dad—I can still remember him hollering when he saw those pictures."

"It was a nice sailor suit and you were only four years old."

"Trust me. It could have been worse."

"What could have been worse?" Rosie laughed.

"No—I—Hell, I never even mentioned it to Elizabeth." He looked at Rosie. She was sitting cross-legged on the front seat like a little girl. She looked so pretty, he thought. "I mean, it never came up. That's why I never mentioned it. I only saw the pictures once. I forgot about them until you mentioned the thing."

"The guy on the television show," Rosie told him, "said that they got the pictures out of an old photo album."

"Album?" It had to be Aunt Dorothy. "Shit." She had to be eighty-five if she was a day, because she'd been a lot older than his mother. He remembered that well enough.

"What kind of picture are you afraid to tell me about, David?"

"I'm not afraid to—"

"Bullshit." Rosie laughed. "What kind of picture was it? Huh? Come on—tell Rosie."

It was the first time he'd ever heard her refer to herself as "Rosie." "Nothing. Don't worry—"

"I'm not worried. You're the one who's worried."

"I'm not worried. For God's sake, I was only four years old and she was—"

"What kind of picture?"

If there had been a gas station he would have stopped to shut her up.

"What kind of picture, David?"

David Holden swallowed. "With a Superman suit on," he mumbled.

"A what?"

"A Superman suit," he mumbled again. "And another with an Easter bunny outfit, and—"

"Oh, my God!"

"All right, there, I said it. Okay. A damn bunny suit, okay?"

"Oh, David. With ears and everything?"

Holden could feel his cheeks getting warm. "All right, yeah. Ears and everything. The whole damn thing."

"Did she have you holding a little Easter basket?"

"No—I can't remember—yeah, I guess so."

"What color?" She giggled.

"It was a black-and-white photograph. How the hell should I know? That was a long time ago. Forget about it," Holden told her.

"You're blushing. My God! You're blushing! I didn't think you could!"

"I'm not blushing. Hot." Holden rolled down the window.

"Aw, I bet you were the cutest bunny!"

"Knock it off," Holden snapped.

"Would you dress up like a bunny—"

"No, dammit!"

"I could call you 'Bunny' for a nickname. Just when we were alone—"

"No," and Holden dug into his pockets, searching for a cigarette.

Rosie was still giggling.

"Shit."

CHAPTER 13

He stopped the Ford and got out, the little .45 in his right hand.

They were well away from the beach, well away from the hotel at Siamese Shoals, and on the far side of the town of Harrington. "What's your real name? I mean, I don't think it's Bart anymore, and you don't sound like a Doctor somebody. What did he call you?"

"Doctor Phillip Ridgely, a name I used."

"What's your real name? I mean, you don't have to really tell me your real name. Just tell me it's real and I'll believe you because I want to, that's all."

"I love you. I don't suppose you'll believe me when I say this, but I've never said that to anyone before and meant it."

"I know that," Linda Effingham told him. "I knew you'd come back for me. And I knew that was why you'd come back for me. That was why I didn't want to be left behind. I mean, I know you'll do what you have to do and go away and I'll never see you again, but you wouldn't have left me like that."

He turned around and looked at her. The moon was very bright. He'd driven by its light alone for the last several miles. "You're right. I wouldn't have left you like that. I couldn't have."

"Are you some kind of policeman or government agent? Or shouldn't I ask?"

"You shouldn't ask."

"Tell me a name I should call you by."

He was supposed to lie, of course. That was standard stuff. The one name for which he didn't have a shred of identification was his own. "Geoff, Geoffrey Kearney."

"That's a nice name. Did you make it up or did—"

"My mother and father made it up, actually"—and he looked away from her, lighting a cigarette in the blue yellow flame of his brass Zippo lighter. "At least they made up the Geoffrey part. Kearney was already there."

"Who are you?"

He loved the sound of her voice. "I told you; I'm Geoffrey Kearney. Call me Geoff if you like, but forget the last name."

"I meant what are you? A policeman? Is the accent real?"

"Where I come from, darling, you have the accent. I'm here for my government. That's all I can say and that says it rather well, really. I expect I'm most similar to a policeman of sorts, yes. And I'm also something like an executioner. You see"—and he inhaled hard on his cigarette—"a sentence of death has been passed on a man. I'm not quite sure which man. But, once I am, then I'm supposed to carry it out. And, to spare your feelings, it doesn't offend mine at all. The fellow deserves to die. So, I expect, I'm a bit like a judge and a jury, in that way. I find him as a policeman, I judge him, I determine his fate if he fits the mold, and then I kill him. You don't belong in a world like that."

"I love you too."

Kearney inhaled on his cigarette. "That's another reason I came back to the bar. This isn't a perfect world, darling. In a perfect world the violins would begin to play"—he looked at the moon, trying to see a face inscribed upon its brilliant white surface, but unable to do so. "And we'd go off to some cottage together and all of that. But there are a lot of men in this world who want to destroy it, just to see if they can. Rather like the child who's given a toy that winds up for Christmas or his birthday and is told, 'Don't turn the key too much, because if you do, your toy will break.' Well, we all know that the child will, after a bit, begin to wind the toy and wind it and wind it and, eventually, if he isn't stopped, the toy will break, the spring sprung. There are people like that in the world, Linda, people who don't believe that if they wind too hard the toy will break, or, worse yet, the ones who don't care if the toy breaks. And there are some, a very few, who really and truly wish that the toy will break, wish for it with all their might and main and every fiber of their being. And they will never be happy as long as the toy remains unbroken."

He turned around and looked at her again, just sitting there in the front seat of the car, hands resting in her lap, his jacket over her beautifully bare shoulders, so exquisite that he could almost get an erection just thinking about her. "So, I suppose one might say that I represent the toy company. I'm here to prevent someone from breaking one, irreplaceable toy. Because if that toy is broken, all the rest of the toys will die. So I have to stop the toy from being broken. And the little boy who thinks he was given the toy—although he really wasn't given it at all—has to be fixed so he can never play with the toy again."

"You talk a lot."

Kearney dropped his cigarette to the ground and stepped on it. "Yes."

"Make love to me. Just in case the little boy breaks the toy before you can find him."

"Yes," Geoffrey Kearney told her.

Linda Effingham stepped out of the car, into his arms.

CHAPTER 14

The fourth stolen car died and they walked, holding hands, for two miles until they reached the turnoff for the camp. The fourth car died a peaceful death. The alternator light came on, the warm smell of roast beef gravy suddenly permeated the interior of the car, and a little, almost cheerful red light illuminated the blackness of the dashboard. Suddenly, as they made a curve and he touched his foot to the brake, the car breathed its last.

Whoever owned it might find it—Holden hoped the person would, because stealing anything made his skin crawl. He left fifty dollars—money was of little use where he was going—in the ashtray, salve for his conscience, money for a new alternator. The car had more gasoline in it than it had had when he and Rosie stole it.

But he knew that whoever would likely find the car would check the car inside and out and probably find the fifty dollars and keep the money. That didn't exactly bother him, because at least he had made the attempt.

Still holding hands, the Desert Eagle stuffed in his trouser band, they walked along the rutted ranch road, toward the camp. Soon they would encounter Patriot sentries, he hoped.

Rosie was crying. It had started very suddenly and was something she rarely did. "What's the matter?"

"My suitcase."

"What do you mean?"

"Remember I told you I bought that pink sundress?"

Holden really didn't remember. He had always tried to be honest. "Pink dress?"

"Yeah." Rosie sniffed. "The one from that French shop in Fortaleza."

He remembered Fortaleza and managed a noncommittal "Oh, yeah!"

"I had it in my bag. It's in the trunk of the damn car."

"The Rolls?"

"Yeah."

"I'm sorry."

"I wanted you to see it on me," she told him, sniffing back tears.

"Thanks for loving me," David Holden told her, stopping in the middle of the rutted ranch road, pulling Rosie into his arms and kissing her hard on the mouth. Her arms folded around his neck. She tasted faintly of salt from her tears.

CHAPTER 15

Rudolph Cerillia had never gone through such a complicated procedure in his life to lose a tail; but as he entered the Castle, he felt confident that the tail was lost.

The museums of the Smithsonian Institution had always been his only love in Washington, the Castle most of all. Its exhibits recalled a gentler age, or at least he perceived it as gentler by being removed from it by the decades and centuries.

He looked at his watch. Between all the complications and the normal Washington traffic being confounded by random searches and roadblocks (and the necessity of avoiding those because he was, unofficially, under house arrest), he was late. If Luther Steel followed the rules, he wouldn't be there anymore.

But Rudolph Cerillia saw him now, tall, black, every inch the athlete, wearing a neatly tailored business suit under his raincoat.

Steel stood beside an exhibit of pristine steel tools from the turn of the century, the steel gleaming as brightly as Cerillia imagined some mythic sword might gleam. Tools were the swords of civilization, Cerillia had often thought, and he liked this exhibit which so glorified them.

Simple tools. Hammers, wrenches, screwdrivers,

tools made to fit into a man's hand and allow him to shape what was to come.

Things were not that simple anymore.

Cerillia came up behind Steel; but, to the FBI agent's credit, Steel turned around. "You've got good hearing Luther." Rudolph Cerillia smiled, extending his hand.

Steel took his hand, saying, "Thank you very much Mr.—"

"Don't you dare call me that." Cerillia smiled, looking over his shoulder.

They released their handclasp, Cerillia passing Luther Steel to step closer to the exhibit. "I've always admired simplicity. Maybe that's why I can't stand airplanes."

"They're simple machines."

Cerillia looked at Steel. "I have to talk quickly. My car will be spotted where I left it at any moment now, and if I'm not back at the house, they'll become even more suspicious than they are now. And I have to stay operational for a little while longer. Here's a list." Cerillia drew a matchbook out of his overcoat pocket and handed it to Steel. "You'll need a powerful magnifying glass to read it. There's a name on each of the matchsticks. If they'd gotten me, I would have lit the whole pack."

"Look. I can get you out of Washington, sir. My men—"

"Your men have more important things to do Luther. I'm gone. It's only a matter of time. The names on that list are men you can trust, men I've trusted as much as our mutual friend Rocky Saddler. You'll need the names of these men, one way or the other."

"I can get you out of here, sir," Steel insisted.

Cerillia had always liked the sound of Steel's voice, confident without being cocky. If he'd had a son, he would have wanted him to be just like Luther Steel. Race had nothing to do with it. "There's a more important man you have to rescue, Luther, more important to all of us. I've received word that the—" And Cerillia looked around them, began walking slowly, Steel falling in beside him. "The President is coming out of his coma. Just some signs, but good ones."

Another thing Rudolph Cerillia had always liked about Luther Steel was his innate honesty. His face read like a book for the visually impaired and his voice could never hide emotion. "That's fantastic!"

"Hold your horses, Luther. It could be fantastic. But not if you know who gets to him first."

"You mean that—"

Cerillia looked around them again, stopping to admire a Rube Goldberg–looking device with flywheels and levers all painted in bright colors. "Roman Makowski won't surrender the Presidency. If he did, the President would have him arrested and tried for treason. And the President still commands the power and the respect to do that. Makowski knows it. Makowski wouldn't just be out of the Oval Office, he'd be out of Washington period, probably in prison. Makowski already knows the President is showing signs of improvement, but he hasn't seen the latest report. I have.

"The President actually spoke. Very slurred, unintelligible, but he actually opened his eyes and he spoke." Cerillia felt his own voice choke with emotion. "Once Makowski learns that, Makowski won't be able to take any chances. He'll have to act at once. As soon as the President is able to show signs of more or less full possession of his faculties—and the latest prognosis is for that and soon—Makowski's out on his ear. So he'll have to act very quickly to assassinate the President or he won't be able to do it at all."

A school group walked past them, and Cerillia fell silent until the last child had passed.

Steel said, "But he couldn't risk—"

"He's risked everything already. The Secret Service, try as they might, won't be able to protect the President, not from a full-blown assault after Makowski pulls away most of the security. The only chance is to get the President out and to safety. You and your people won't be enough manpower. You'll have to get Holden's people, the Patriots. And pray to God Holden himself is back. This will all have to be done very quickly. The President—now, memorize this—isn't at Bethesda as the press has been saying. He's at a private hospital in Virginia, Pinewood Sanitorium. Full staff. He's the only patient. Used to be run by the CIA years ago as a recuperation center for agents. There's air security and ground security. Talk to Chester Welles. He's on that list I gave you. He knows the place. You'll have to get the President out before Makowski can kill him. You have hours, not days, to get that done."

"What about you, sir?"

Rudolph Cerillia took Steel's hand in his, looking at the younger man square in the eye. "I'm a marked man. It's only a matter of time. If I vanished now,

Makowski'd know I'm onto him. And then he might accelerate his plans to get the President. But if they get me, I've got a little surprise for them. Maybe, if you and Holden can pull this off, maybe we'll put things right again." And Cerillia still held Luther Steel's right hand in his. "In case I don't make it, well—God bless you, son"—and Rudolph Cerillia released Luther Steel's hand and walked back past the tool display.

He wanted to see that one more time, for some reason he himself didn't quite understand.

CHAPTER 16

David Holden was very tired, but Patsy Alfredi and the other Patriots were very eager. And so, with Rosie beside him, they sat around the fire in the cool night air, Holden recounting—although skipping some of the more painful details—what had transpired since he had been kidnapped, including a much-watered-down version of the torture session with Borsoi. He had told Rosie all the details and she'd held him in her arms. But he would never tell anyone else.

Eventually the fire began to die and with it, it seemed, the curiosity.

They returned to their tent.

"I kept these for you," Rosie told him, going into the suitcase he used as a footlocker, taking from it two lumpy packages wrapped in rags. He unfolded the rags and the shapes became more distinct. At last he exposed his two Beretta pistols. "And I used this. I kind of needed to as a sort of badge of authority with you gone."

"There's nothing I can do that you can't do at least as well," Holden told Rosie Shepherd honestly.

She handed him the Desert Eagle. "Good to have you back, boss." She smiled.

"Good to be back." David Holden set aside his guns and his knife, the new Desert Eagle beside them. He couldn't quite see himself carrying two Desert

Eagles into combat and still walking, considering the combined weight of the rest of his gear, but his opinion on that might always change.

His clothes were all washed and folded, everything ready for his return. When he looked at Rosie—he supposed a little oddly—she smiled and said, "Gave me something to do."

He took Rosie into his arms and they dropped to their knees on the ground. After a while he'd wash up, she would unroll the blankets, and they'd hold each other for a while until the blankets warmed to their bodies and they would make love.

But for now David Holden just held Rosie very close.

CHAPTER 17

Luther Steel kept the matchbook in the left inside breast pocket of his suit coat.

There was no time now to magnify and transcribe the names listed on the matchsticks. But he could not risk losing them either.

The flight out of Dulles was uneventful. Again, he hadn't used his badge as identification and he traveled weaponless. But to intentionally draw attention to his travels would be risking . . . He couldn't bring himself to think of that so specifically. To be arrested just because he was, at the moment, politically objectionble was nauseating even to consider. This was the United States of America, not some communist country where honest citizens couldn't come and go as they pleased.

He read the newspaper, which was even more depressing after the long lines for the searches of person and luggage he'd had to endure before boarding the double-entry bus that took him from the gate to the aircraft.

The newspaper was filled with stories of arrests, and despite the almost gleeful tone of the reports, it seemed evident many of the arrests had been wrongful, all of them because of Executive Order 128946. All in the quest for stealing, in the name of the law, firearms privately owned by honest citizens.

Somehow this would make America safer, the

obviously biased tone of the newspaper articles went, by incarcerating and fining honest citizens for keeping their previously legally owned possessions.

The NRA and the Citizens Committee were taking the government to court in separate legal actions. The report concerning this was very small and buried near the obituaries, the writer of the article—there was no byline—intimating that this was another attempt by the "gun lobby" to keep killer weapons in the hands of criminals and to foil the efforts of police in their attempts to stop terrorism and violence.

There was no mention of the innocent lives privately owned firearms had protected since the violence had begun. Like most career law-enforcement personnel, as opposed as he was to politically motivated management functionaries, he had always generally favored access to firearms for private citizens. Aside from the basis for this right in the Bill of Rights, it was practical; the worse crime became, the more practical private firearms ownership became. It was impossible for the law to guard every citizen's home one on one. With that impossibility as a given and the reality that even 911 calls might not bring police assistance for tens of minutes or longer, what were private citizens to do? Die with smiles on their faces knowing they had obeyed a law made by men who didn't have to worry about self-defense because they could afford high-security residences, chauffeurs with counterterrorist driving training, and bodyguards who might even be equipped with automatic weapons?

There was something very wrong.

Managed news? Steel wondered, but in the final

analysis concluded that Roman Makowski was just the sort of man much of the liberal media, print and electronic, had been trying to get into office for decades. And the media would ride with him, support him, no matter how illogical that seemed to persons of different mind-sets. Makowski would have all the support he needed until he began to muzzle the newspaper and the television networks. Then, when they no longer had the power to inform, to educate, to stimulate thinking, they would react.

Too late.

It was almost too late now.

If Makowski had the real President assassinated, "too late" would have arrived.

When the plane landed at Metro, Steel was at greatest risk of being recognized. He'd instructed Randy Blumenthal, who had the lowest profile of all of the now officially disbanded and all-but-outlawed Metro task force, to meet him.

Blumenthal, too, was without badge and gun.

"I've got bad news, Mr. Steel," he said, as they shook hands just outside the internal security area. There were random checks now of passengers and baggage as they entered the terminal, in addition to the now-traditional scanning and more detailed searches of carryon luggage.

Steel said nothing, just walked beside him through the airport lobby toward baggage claim. People were pushing, shoving, and some were running to get to the next line where they would have to wait and wait until they were cleared and could escape the terminal or board their flights. Steel had no baggage, but baggage claim was the quickest exit to the street.

"It was on the wire. Bill got it."

"What was on the wire?"

"We've been officially declared absent from our new assignments and suspended without pay. Just Bill and Clark and Tom and me. Nothing about you, so far. And there's supposed to be an internal memorandum going out that we're wanted for questioning—but nothing about you again—for the gunfight at that farm where Hodges was killed."

"Sometimes I wonder who's running things, don't you?" Luther Steel could hardly believe the words were coming from his own lips. "I mean, we're trying to enforce the law and we're wanted for questioning for doing it. Doesn't make a lot of sense. But what does?" Doing your duty didn't mean you had to expect to be appreciated, Steel reminded himself.

They passed into the baggage claim area after waiting in a long line. The lines were just as long as at any other exit but they usually moved faster. "Baggage to claim?" The female security guard, black like Steel and looking rather silly in a Sam Browne belt that diagonally bisected her torso between the breasts, addressed the question to both of them.

"He's meeting me. I only have this attaché case," Steel told her.

"Let's open it up."

Steel looked at her for an instant, then turned toward the inspection table, unlocking and opening his attaché case. In it were the newspaper he'd read, a paperback adventure novel, a Washington, D.C., city map, a spare shirt, handkerchief, and underpants and pair of socks, for just in case. There was also a Swiss Army Champion pocketknife.

"What's this?"

"A Swiss Army knife. They comply with FAA regulations to the best of my knowledge. I usually carry it in my pocket."

"They may be legal aboard the aircraft, but they aren't legal in the terminal. The knife has to be surrendered or you're under arrest."

Steel closed his eyes, took a deep breath. "Ma'am. I'm in the process of leaving the airport."

"The rules are the rules. If you wish, you can file a contraband confiscation claim and appeal to the airport authority to hold the knife while you take it up with the city's department of public safety."

"All that for a little knife?"

"There's a lot of people in line behind you. What's it gonna be?"

Steel would have loved to show his badge and pull rank. But he didn't have his badge and what was the average guy supposed to do? "Take the damn knife."

"Look. I don't have to take you using foul language."

"I'm sorry," he lied.

"Guys like you give all of us a bad name," she snapped, taking the knife. "Want a recovery appeal form?"

"No. I'll buy a new knife."

"Won't do you any good to travel with it. Go on through." Steel just looked at her for a moment, then caught up his attaché case and closed it. Steel started to walk away with Blumenthal behind him. "Wait a minute!"

Steel stopped, didn't turn around. "Yes?"

"You'll need a pass so that case won't have to be inspected again. Here."

Steel turned around, walked back, took the offered pass. "Thank you."

She just turned away.

Luther Steel rejoined Randy Blumenthal and walked on. . . .

He slid into the front seat beside Clark Pietrowski. "Clark, good to see you. Tom. Bill? How are you feeling?"

"I limp a little and I don't look forward to doing much running. Other than that, I'm okay, boss."

Steel nodded to Runningdeer. Pietrowski was already turning into traffic. "I'm glad you guys got out of there. I was listening to the cops on the radio," Pietrowski said slowly, lighting a cigarette, letting it hang from the left corner of his mouth. He turned onto the outgoing traffic ramp. "Guess which bullet from which dead man was finally matched to somebody's gun, that same lucky somebody spotted earlier today in Metro and wanted for questioning on suspicion of murder?"

"Aw, shit," Randy Blumenthal groaned.

"Bingo! I got it all figured, though." Pietrowski laughed, putting on his signal and blending into the expressway traffic. "We hold on to Randy until they make a reward offer for the insane killer of that upstanding citizen Humphrey Hodges. So, who cares Hodges was working with the FLNA and working with

Dimitri Borsoi, right? Hey! Then, we turn in Randy and—"

"Enough, Clark," Luther Steel hissed. He'd had more than enough of a lot of things. "We have to get in touch with the Patriots, see if Holden was found. Mr. Cerillia told me the President spoke, actually spoke."

"Thank God!" Tom LeFleur almost shouted.

"Yeah"—Steel nodded—"but the trouble is that with the prognosis they're making now for the President to be restored enough to health that he can resume his office, Mr. Cerillia has reason to believe Roman Makowski'll make the move to have the President assassinated. And very quickly. We have a contact name who's supposedly familiar with the facility where the President is being kept."

"I thought he was at Bethesda," Clark Pietrowski interrupted.

"That was just for the media, Clark. It's a place called Pinewood Sanitorium in Virginia. Used to be a CIA R-and-R location. I've been given a whole list of people we can count on. Mr. Cerillia," Steel almost whispered, looking down at his hands, "seems convinced that Makowski will probably nail him, kill him."

"We can—" Runningdeer began, but stopped.

Steel didn't say anything for a long moment, watching the traffic, watching the lights of the approaching cars. Then he said what hung on the air. "We can't. Because it would speed up things against the President. That's pretty much the way Mr. Cerillia told it to me. And he's right. But if we can get the President to safety, we can try getting Mr. Cerillia out. Which makes for more urgency. But we'll need the

elp of the Patriots for manpower. That was Mr. Ceril-
ia's direction. And I intend we carry it out."

"Here," Bill Runningdeer said.

Steel turned around, looking into the backseat.
Runningdeer held Steel's DeSantis shoulder holster
with Steel's SIG-Sauer P-226 in it. "You'll be needing
his."

Steel took the gun and holster and started to shrug
ut of his suit coat.

CHAPTER 18

Lem Parrish noticed that the red light on the telephone was blinking, put down his earphones, and picked up the receiver. "Yeah."

"Somebody outside to see you. Black guy. Know him?"

"You gotta be more specific. I know a lot of black people."

Automatically he checked the studio clock. Four more minutes on the news. He was filling in for the two-until-six shift. The woman who usually spun records and swapped carts in and out of the players had been mugged and almost raped the previous night and was at home. She needed the time off and Parrish had convinced himself he could get along on a little less sleep. It was sort of like the old days, just the idle, trivial DJ chatter and the records and a lot of time to read, and a lot of coffee to drink.

The night security guard's voice came back through the receiver. "Say's his name is Luther. Won't gimme a last name."

Parrish swallowed hard. Luther Steel. "Let him come up. He's an old buddy. Don't bother wanding him."

"Hey—I got my orders, Mr. Parrish."

"Yeah, and I can still get you fired, Joe. Let him up."

There was a pause for a beat and a half, then, "So all right, already."

He eyed the studio clock, set the record on the turntable to his right, found the right cut, and rotated the turntable clockwise and counterclockwise until he had the right spot and it was cued.

There was a knock at the door. "Come on in." He glanced at the clock again, then at the door as Luther Steel stepped through the doorway. "Close it behind you, Luther. Good to see you."

"We've got to talk."

"Two minutes before the news."

"Is it safe to talk here?"

Parrish grinned. "Safe to talk here? Hell, where's it safe? But we're soundproofed and I won't open a microphone for better than a minute and a half, so it's as safe as anyplace else."

"The President is on the road to recovery."

Parrish almost fell out of his chair. "You're jivin' me!"

"No. But there's an assassination plot against him, we think, and I need David Holden's help."

"He may not even be back yet."

"Hope to God he is. We need manpower we can trust. And we need it fast. Can you get me to their camp?"

"Sure. As soon as I'm off the air. That's another two hours."

"No time for that," Steel said.

Lem Parrish eyed the clock on the wall. "Hold on a little." He watched the second hand, put his earphones back on and caught the sign-off, then keyed his microphone. "This is Lem Parrish sitting in for Daphne of the Night with the mellow sounds of the old Velvet Fog, Mel Torme, singing 'Autumn in New York.' Hey, it's gotta beat autumn in Metro, huh?" And he started the record.

He threw down his earphones and picked up the receiver of his telephone, punching to an outgoing line. He waited and waited. "Daphne?"

Her voice sounded terrible.

"I know you feel like shit," he told her. "You gotta help me. I'm sending over a tall, good-looking guy to pick you up and bring you over here. he's a cop, sort of. You'll be safe with him. I've gotta split, but I'll be back before you get off the air and I'll take you home. Can you do it?"

She told him something he should do to himself sexually, then laughed a little and told him okay.

"Good. He's leaving now. Black guy named Luther. Trust him. Thanks, babes." He hung up and rotated his chair toward Luther Steel. "You know the area just above the bypass near the restaurant strip where they've got the Highlight Bar?"

Steel looked as though he didn't.

"Well," Parrish told him, "you're about to have a geography lesson." He took out a sheet of paper and started drawing a map. "Her name's Daphne and she's a knockout."

CHAPTER 19

Rosie awakened in David's arms to Mort Levine's voice outside the tent. "Hey, Rosie." Mort was in charge of camp security and that translated to supervising the guard details and, if someone couldn't make his post, finding somebody who could. She would volunteer for guard detail sometimes, as would David, mostly because Mort never assigned them. She'd asked him once why not and he'd said, "Heck, Rosie, you guys are the leaders. The leaders aren't supposed to draw guard detail. Did General Patton ever draw guard detail?"

"When I start carrying two ivory-handled revolvers and I grow balls, I'll let you know, okay?"

But she had respected his wishes, merely volunteering instead, as did David.

"What's up, Mort?"

"Lem Parrish and that FBI agent, Steel, are out over by the fire and need to see you and David right away. Real urgent."

"Wonderful." She sat up, David awake beside her. "You hear?"

"Yeah. I guess we really are back home. Business as usual, huh?" And he put his arms around her and she let him kiss her really hard and didn't want him to stop. But he let her go, stood up, and grabbing up his underpants, pulled them on. Then he stepped into his pants and started looking for his other combat boot.

She got out from between the covers and was instantly covered with gooseflesh. She had the luxury of a bathrobe and she was glad for it, pulling it on around her, standing up, stuffing her feet into her track shoes, wriggling her toes to get into the shoes without having to untie them. She was still cold. David pulled a black Woolly Pully over his head. She'd been planning on wearing that, so she grabbed up an M-65 field jacket instead. It was his, but that didn't matter. She just threw it over her shoulders, hugging it around her as she followed him out of the tent.

She noticed he had the Desert Eagle she'd brought to him inside the waist band of his BDU pants as he pulled the sweater over it. She smiled. She'd caught up the Glock-17, chamber empty, and stuffed it in the pocket of the field jacket.

She walked beside David toward what remained of the fire.

Luther Steel's broad shoulders and generally athletic build were unmistakable and, anyway, he was one of the few people she knew who almost invariably wore a suit and tie. Lem Parrish, his left hand out of sight as it almost always was, stood beside Steel.

"Luther. Lem," Rosie called out.

"Hiya, Rosie," Lem called back. "See you got our boy back, huh?"

"My boy. You find your own." Rosie Shepherd laughed.

David stopped a foot or so away from Steel and Lem Parrish and they went through the man-thing of shaking hands and nodding and not saying anything for a few seconds.

"So," Rosie began. "What's up?"

"There may be a plot afoot to—"

" 'Afoot,' Luther? What the hell movie you—"

"I'm serious, Detective Shepherd," Luther Steel said quietly. "There may be a plot to assassinate the President because he's coming out of his coma and is expected to survive, and we need the help of the Patriots."

She looked for a place to sit down, found a folding camp chair, and sank down into it, wishing she'd brought her cigarettes.

CHAPTER 20

It was steamy hot outside and the contrast with the air conditioning of the lobby made his sweated-through white shirt instantly begin to dry against his back. The lobby ceiling was high and vaulted, reminiscent of the Turkish style used during the Ottoman Empire and decorated with intricate patterns of ceramic tile almost perfectly matching the design in the floor so that if one stared at the ceiling long enough it was easy to become slightly disoriented, even dizzy. Tom Ashbrooke had no time for staring at ceilings; all he gave it was a glance.

He crossed the hall and took the stairs to the left rear. As he reached a height of ten or twelve feet, the oppressive heat returned.

The building had been erected during the British occupation of what was then known as Palestine and was not designed for central air conditioning. Indeed only the first-floor hall had air conditioning to this day.

He became progressively hotter and hotter, sweating again, which chilled him, only differently from before. Each night after he would return from another interrogation session with Emiliano Ortega de Vasquez, before a late dinner, even before calling his wife, Diane, he would pour a glass of iced tea or occasionally a lightly mixed screwdriver or salty dog, then sit in the bathtub to equalize his body temperature.

Then he took a shower, but only after a long time in the tub. Then he placed the nightly call to Diane.

Ashbrooke stopped at the landing, looked down, drew a breath, and tackled the next flight. He prided himself on being fit, but at his age there was no sense pushing his luck. But he took the stairs quickly, almost at a jog.

There was a long corridor floored with small, chipping black-and-white tiles with occasional black patches where they'd been less than artfully repaired. He walked toward the steel door at the far end and knocked. He was running late, but there had been business matters to take care of, some stock transfers and the like.

The door was opened by the woman with the pockmarked, but otherwise pretty, face. She pushed her shoulder-length auburn waves back, smiling with her huge brown eyes and her wide mouth. "Mr. Ashbrooke. We were beginning to think you might not come."

"Wouldn't miss it." He smiled back.

She opened the door wider and he stepped through the doorway and into the windowless interrogation room. It was built to withstand bomb blasts, and if, perish the thought, the air conditioning in the room (the unit had been mounted through the wall and was armor plated) should fail and the door became stuck, they would all suffocate.

"Señor Ortega de Vasquez is in a talkative mood today." Hugo Krakowski's blue eyes smiled.

"Are you?" Ashbrooke remarked cheerfully. "Well, that's wonderful. It would be terrible if we just put you out on the street and let it be known how you sacrificed Innocentio Hernandez and told us everything you know about the drug cartel and the international terrorist underground."

Krakowski laughed and so did the girl, Helen. But Ortega de Vasquez didn't.

Slowly, over the days of interrogation since they'd brought him to Israel, both his dapper appearance and confident demeanor had begun to fade.

"Tell Mr. Ashbrooke what you told us, Emiliano," Hugo Krakowski said in an amiable voice. He sucked on his empty pipe. Sweat had beaded on his high forehead and was visible in the thinning crew-cut on top of his head.

"The People for a Better America, the lobbying group that is tied up very closely to the American President, is headed by Horace Elderton. He is part of the Front for the Liberation of North America, I think."

Tom Ashbrooke sat down on one of the folding chairs, his sport coat over his arm. He was perspiring profusely, the air conditioning's effect lost to him. "What do you mean that you think he is?"

"His assistant, Señorita Nancy O'Donnell, was the mistress of Dimitri Borsoi before she—"

"Dimitri Borsoi," Ashbrooke repeated under his breath.

"*Sí*. This Señorita O'Donnell. She was Borsoi's paramour and then she became Elderton's assistant. Maybe she sleeps with both men, hey?"

Dimitri Borsoi through Nancy O'Donnell, whoever the hell she was, had a direct link to Roman Makowski. Thomas Ashbrooke felt sick to his stomach.

CHAPTER 21

The house looked like pictures of old Victorian English country homes she had seen in magazines or in movies. Vines—starting to die out for the season—clung to the irregular stone surfaces surrounding the doorway. Rose Shepherd walked between David and Luther Steel. Steel's car (with Bill Runningdeer at the wheel) sat parked in the horseshoe-shaped gravel driveway fronting the house.

It was becoming increasingly difficult to travel. Conventional air transportation was out, of course, and ground transportation could take forever because of the problem of avoiding roadblocks, which were increasingly random, almost impromptu.

They had utilized the cargo plane of Chester Little, that talkative little devil who had flown her and David out to New Mexico and back when they'd gone there with Steel and gotten involved with the FLNA attack on the security conference. She smiled when she thought of him, Little so overtly macho, so tight lipped, but a nice guy anyway.

David remarked to her as they began to ascend the steps to the doorway, "For once the old line is appropriate."

"What old line, David?"

"You're a Rose between two thorns."

The wood-paneled door, set with small panes of

107

stained glass, opened before they reached the top step.
"I'm Chester Welles. I recognize your picture, Professor Holden, and I recognize you from the description
Rudy Cerilla gave me. Agent Steel. And this lovely
lady in green, I presume, is the notorious Detective
Rose Shepherd." He was tall, but not extraordinarily
so, had thick, close-cut gray hair, character lines in his
face—the sort of thing that would be called wrinkles in
a woman—and clear blue eyes.

She was wearing green, all right, lime-green. It
was a dress with a collar that stood up at the back, cut
like a man's shirt, a little fabric belt tied around the
waist, and a full skirt that moved when she did. And it
was nice of him to say she was lovely, but he probably
would have said that if she were homely enough to
make somebody throw up just looking at her.

David extended his hand as he mounted the last
step. "A pleasure to meet you, Mr. Welles."

"Same here." Luther Steel nodded, next in line
for the handshake.

Rosie stuck out her own hand and he took her
hand just as he would have taken a man's hand, not just
the fingers as though he were about to kiss her hand or
something. She liked that.

"Come on in, people. Catch a lot of things standing around talking on porches, including a cold." It was
warm in the direct sunlight, despite the cool temperatures. He ushered them through the doorway, Rose
first, then closed the door after them. She shrugged
the white sweater off her shoulders, David helping her
with it. It was impossible to wear her shoulder holster
under her dress, but the Detonics Servicemaster .45

was in her purse and she didn't intend to let go of the purse, no matter how nice this Chester Welles appeared. "There's coffee in the library and stronger beverages, too, for anyone of a mind. I understand you people need me to draw some pictures and answer some questions."

"We need to know everything you can tell us about Pinewood Sanitorium," Luther Steel said, coming right to the point.

"As you probably understand, it's very important, important that we get every detail you can think of," David added.

Welles laughed as he guided them into the study. "Well, the food was really bad there in 1944, but I imagine that's changed. I was there when I was in OSS—although I didn't know I was in OSS at the time, just thought I was in some special branch of Naval Intelligence—and I was there again in 1968 and in 1984. I have no idea what's been done to the place since, but I can tell you everything I remember."

The study or library was the perfect man's room, Rose thought. Dark, rich-looking paneling covered two walls, the third wall dominated by French doors opening, she supposed, to a patio or garden. In the fourth wall was a massive hearth of flagstone, a fire burning in it. Beside the hearth, near a brass-studded maroon leather easy chair and matching ottoman, lay a dog. The animal should have been an Irish setter but was a very peaceful-looking coal-black Doberman instead. Above the mantel was hung a flintlock rifle (it looked to be genuine, not a replica or reproduction) and a powder horn, on the other walls an assortment of edged weapons, seemingly genuine as well, swords of various styles, what she thought was called a halberd, and knives of almost every description. Other leather furniture, comfortable looking, was dotted about the room. Bookshelves were built in everywhere, some books even spilling over onto the fireplace mantel, a few on the shelves behind the bar that dominated the corner abutting the wall with the patio doors. A pipe rack was beside the leather easy chair. As Chester Welles walked toward the chair, the Doberman rose lazily, stretched—he had to be over standard size for his breed—and sauntered over to lie down again beside the ottoman, nearer to his master.

"Please. I'm not a gracious enough host to fix drinks, just offer them. Bar's over there. Coffee's there too."

"I'll get whatever anybody wants," Rose volunteered. She only volunteered because she assumed such was socially expected of anyone foolish enough to grow up with breasts instead of testicles.

"I'll be the first to take you up on your kind offer," Welles said, also as she'd expected.

She started to gravitate toward the bar. "What'll ya have, Mr. Welles?" What if he wanted something really complicated or exotic?

"Just two fingers of Canadian Club and three ice cubes."

That was simple enough. "David?"

"Coffee."

"Luther?"

"Coffee."

She wondered if she'd get a tip. She started finding

cups and glasses. She wasn't driving and there wouldn't be any shooting or anything until nightfall. He had some good stuff. She decided on making herself a cuba libre, like Tom Ashbrooke had taught her about, except there didn't seem to be any limes. "The hell with the lime."

"What?" David asked.

"Nothing." She smiled cheerfully.

She listened as the men talked. "Let's get the cards on the table, Professor, Agent Steel. I know the President is probably at Pinewood Sanitorium. You don't have to lie and say he isn't or violate a confidence and say he is. And, I suppose Roman Makowski is planning to move on him."

"Luther? Cream or sugar?"

"Black."

Somehow Rose had known that would be his answer. And she already knew David took his coffee black.

There was Myer's dark rum and there was Coca-Cola and she started mixing.

"If you were right, Mr. Welles," David was saying, "then you can appreciate how every detail can be important." There was ice in a small bar refrigerator.

"I drive by there every now and again. I was in love with a nurse there in 1944. Hell of a gal. Kind of looked like Detective Shepherd there, only not as tall." How tall was she? Rose thought. Not the nurse from 1944, but herself. Too tall? She wasn't having a good day. "Anyway, they've got a lot of security. I'll assume if Makowski's planning to have the President killed, he'll pull as much of that as he can get away with. You guys will have to contend with it too. So, there's only one thing to do. That's why I brought up the nurse. I can't remember her name." That was a hell of a thing to say, Rose thought. Finished with the drinks, she looked around for a tray or something to carry them on. "But we used to go down into the basement sometimes. And we found a passageway. I learned later the passageway was built when there was a scare that Nazi commandos might hit the place to kill important intelligence operatives staying there. So they built a secret passageway leading under the front lawn and coming out by a side road. Not too many people alive would remember it and it wouldn't have been in the drawings for the building because it was an afterthought. May be some DOD records on it someplace, but Makowski probably wouldn't know about them. Now, they could have closed it up, but I don't think so."

She gave up, taking the two cups of coffee, carrying them out on their saucers and bending over to hand one to David, who was siting on the leather couch, and to Steel, on the same couch but at the far other end.

Both men nodded but said nothing. At least David smiled.

She went back to the bar. "This passageway," Luther Steel began. "How big is it?" She got Welles's drink and her own, again walked across the room, handing Welles his drink. He nodded too. Men liked to nod. She took her drink and sat on the couch dead center between David and Luther.

"The passageway is walkable height, if that's what you mean. Either of you guys would probably have to bend over a little. Men weren't generally as tall better

han forty years ago. The way into the basement may
ave been bricked up, so you'd need some tools or
xplosives, depending on how obvious you can afford
o be and how good your demolitions man is."

David asked, "Could we get a dozen men in full
quipment through there?"

"If you were very quiet. When I heard you were
oming, I started digging through my old photo al-
ums. I took a lot of pictures of Pinewood because of
he girl. You see, I didn't have a picture of her, and I
oved her more than I ever loved any other woman.
eeing Pinewood sort of reminds me of her." His voice
eemed to catch a little. "She died in a jeep accident
ix months later. I never married."

Rose Shepherd suddenly felt like crying. And she
idn't feel bad about having gotten the drinks. David
oved her like that. And that made her feel even more
ike crying.

CHAPTER 22

The police were looking for him and for Linda Effingham, and changing license plates on the Ford was only a stopgap measure at best. From a pay telephone at an abandoned convenience store near the town of Harrington, Geoffrey Kearney placed a collect call to Phillip Carlysle, the resident agent he'd worked with a short time ago, at the safe house near Chicago.

Carlysle answered guardedly, but when the operator transmitted the code name Kearney had given her, "Thomas Rule," he accepted the charges.

They spoke in trivialities for better than a minute until Kearney felt certain that the operator, no matter how nosy, would be off the line. "Do you have access to police and Federal wires?" Kearney asked.

"Most of the time, old man. I say—"

"I need to know just how hot I am. There was a gunfight at a hotel that I was staying at. The hotel is called Siamese Shoals and it's near Harrington, North Carolina. I've taken some routine precautions, but that may not be enough. And there's a girl, innocent bystander, but she may be in considerable trouble as well. The point is, I have to know."

"I'll do what I can, old man. How can I reach you?"

"I'll reach you. Is an hour enough time?"

"Yes. Should be."

Kearney hung up.

Linda Effingham sat in the car. He imagined she was terrified and very tired. They'd spent the night sleeping in the car and there'd been no way to shower or change, and unless she borrowed some of his things, there was nothing for her to change into. Routinely Kearney would keep a bag with the basic necessities—black Levi's jeans, shirts, underwear, a couple of sweaters, his leather jacket, and the standard personal items—hidden in the car when he stayed at a hotel for business purposes, as had been the case with Siamese Shoals. The credit cards he had would take care of reoutfitting him with whatever additional attire he might need. And could purchase things for Linda, as well, but the trick there was getting in and out of a store without getting arrested.

He had to know.

Kearney rejoined Linda, sliding in behind the wheel of the Ford. "I reached my friend. I'll call him back after a while and he should be able to give me some word on our situation. Can you make it awhile longer? You've been very brave."

"I'm a little hungry." She smiled.

Kearney could have lived off the land quite nicely around this part of the world, everything from rabbits to birds capable of being snared with a little diligence and planning. But she wasn't the sort of girl who ate things she'd just seen living—lobster probably the exception—and her high heels weren't the best thing for knocking about the woods. "Yes, food would be rather nice. Let's say we try finding a McDonald's or something and use the drive-through window. Arrange your hair a bit differently. You drive and I'll be the passenger. If we get spotted and don't get caught, I can change license plates again."

"Do you think we could?"

"The more I think about it"—Kearney smiled, taking her hand in his—"the more hungry I feel. Let's."

It was a dumb idea, but she was hungry and they'd likely get away with it.

He threw the selector into drive and pulled away from the convenience-store parking lot. . . .

Kearney was eating his second quarter-pound cheeseburger and was already through with a large packet of what Americans insisted on calling "french fries." But a rose by any other name, he told himself— and they tasted good. Linda Effingham was nibbling her way through her first cheeseburger and Kearney held out hope that she wouldn't even try eating her second one at all but insist that he have it, which he would at first decline and, relenting, consume.

There hadn't been even so much as an odd look directed toward them when they'd pulled into the drive-through lane, not from the young black woman who'd taken their money and handed them back their bagged food or—he'd silently thanked God—from the state police officers exiting the restaurant just as he and Linda were driving away.

There should have been a second look, because although the license plates were changed, the color of the Ford was unchanged and the police bulletins should have put law officers in the area on the lookout for such a car with a male and a female subject as occupants.

Nothing.

He wasn't about to try the same telephone, and by the time he found another pay phone that looked as though it might work, nearly an hour and a half had passed.

He rang up Carlysle again, sipping on his chocolate shake as the operator placed the call.

Again they went through the ritual of idle chitchat, this time a bit longer because what Carlysle might say could be potentially more sensitive. Finally, when Kearney thought enough time had elapsed, he asked, "How hot are we?"

"You're not hot at all, old man. There is nothing on the Federal wires concerning any sort of gunfight whatsoever, nor concerning you or a young lady. I tried, through an old acquaintance, on checking the North Carolina state police. There is nothing on any shooting incident anything like what you had described. I think, old man, either you're imagining your involvement in the matter or, for some reason, it may never have been reported. Certainly not out of the county in which it occurred."

"Thank you, my friend. Best to your wife." Kearney hung up. He'd owe Carlysle for that one.

Still sucking on his chocolate shake, Kearney walked along the sidewalk toward where he'd parked the car. Linda was sitting inside.

A police car—state police—was coming down the street, slowly, but not too slowly. Kearney sucked at his shake. He'd shaved with an electric razor powered through an adapter that ran off the cigarette lighter. His tie was straight, his coat neat enough. One of the policemen even looked right at him. Nothing.

Kearney reached the car. Linda was in the passenger seat, her face less than artfully hidden by an open newspaper.

As Kearney rapped on the window with his knuckles, she literally jumped. She put down the newspaper, reached across to unlock his door, and sagged back into the seat. "Those policemen. They scared me to death."

Kearney noticed what she'd been pretending to read, one of the syndicated advice columnists. "She have any words of wisdom for us?" Linda said nothing, so Kearney assumed not. "We're getting out of the county. Driving about a hundred miles or so to be well clear of it. Then we'll find a really nice motel, we can bathe, you tell me what you'll need and I'll find a shop to fill your needs. We're safe."

"What?"

Kearney started the Ford's engine. "Nothing about the affair at Siamese Shoals has been let out of the county, which means that the police in this county are working with the Front for the Liberation of North America, and it's more important to them to conceal the fact that men associated with the Dumbrowski brothers were involved in a gunfight at the hotel than it is to find us. I'll get you home as quickly as possible."

"What about you?" Linda asked him.

"I have a job to do."

"Do you have to get me home that quickly, Geoff?"

Kearney took her into his arms. "I do have that job

to do. And I care for you too much to put you into any more danger than you've already been through."

"I don't care, not if I'm with you."

"But you see, there's the trouble. I would care and I'd be so busy worrying over you that I wouldn't get my job done properly." Under other circumstances he might have been tempted to think about the private security offers he'd gotten over the last few years. The money was vastly better, and so were the hours than his current job and private work would allow him—a lifestyle that had room in it for a woman, maybe more than that. But the world had changed very abruptly in a very short period of time. What had festered under the surface was out in open view and spreading. "It won't be good-bye, if you don't want it to be. But I can't promise anything either. The job I have to do won't be an easy one and it may take some time, actually a lot of time. And there's always the chance—" No, he thought, it would be silly, even maudlin, telling her that. "But it's a job I have to do. Maybe after that, if we're both the same—I don't know."

"Couldn't we just go somewhere?"

"Very few safe places left in the world. Maybe Switzerland, for the time being. But what's happening here is just the tip of the iceberg, as they say, and it won't go away, even if I'm successful at what I have to do."

"You have to find somebody in this Front for—with the terrorists, don't you?"

"They're not terrorists, although many of them were. They use terror as a tactic. They're revolutionaries. And they picked the strongest nation on earth as their first target, and if this nation falls—and it looks as though it might—then all the other democracies will fall. And there'll be no place safe anywhere."

She began to cry. Geoffrey Kearney just held her tightly. If crying would have done any good, he might have been tempted to try it himself.

CHAPTER 23

The side road was within the normal security boundary of the sanitorium grounds, and the prospect of dealing with Secret Service and Marine Corps personnel who were on the same side they were was not something any of them—Steel's FBI team or the hastily assembled group of Patriots—looked forward to. But it was very real.

For the purpose, however, the Patriots in the Alexandria, Virginia, area, with whom Holden and the others would work, had a handy solution. With the abundance of government personnel in the metroplex surrounding Washington, D.C., it had become necessary early on to have a nonlethal way to incapacitate a man temporarily. Two of the Patriots, who had worked at the National Zoo, in conjunction with a Patriot doctor, developed the methodology. The doctor had been at the frontiers of anesthesiological research before he'd been arrested for beating to death an FLNA killer with a chair, (The FLNAer had just murdered the doctor's receptionist with a straight razor across the throat) and the two ex–National Zoo workers had been Patriots from the beginning.

Their system involved CO_2-powered capture-style dart guns. The darts were small hypodermics and the mixture these injected was so powerful a euphoria-inducing compound that the target person passed out with a smile on his face within ten seconds of being injected. The mixture was without danger of heart or respiratory complications and had none of the restrictions of size, weight, and/or age usually attendant to "sleep darts," as such items were sometimes called in popular fiction.

When Holden had learned of the system, its effects were described to him as roughly comparable to chugging an entire bottle of vodka, but without any of the dangerous side effects intrinsic to such massive consumption of alcohol in so short a period of time.

Holden placed an order for a supply of the darts and a few of the pistols, seeing them to be of potential value in Metro, and the leaders of the Alexandria Patriot cell agreed to try to fill it as soon as possible.

They moved along the access road, acutely aware of the fact they were in enemy territory and at any moment might be spotted by a security helicopter or intercepted by a ground patrol. They used three vans, the force of eighteen insertion personnel and three drivers equally divided.

Holden, Rosie Shepherd, Luther Steel, and three of the Alexandria Patriot leadership committee were in the lead van, the man at the wheel also a member of the Alexandria Patriot cell. In the last several weeks six Patriot missions in the D.C. metroplex area had been blown and had met with FLNA ambushes resulting in twenty-seven deaths and the capture of a dozen more Patriots. The Alexandria cell's camp was moved three times.

"I sort of serve as the unofficial advisor on mayhem for the Patriots around the D.C. area, Doctor Holden,"

Chester Welles had told him when, together, at Welles's request, they'd taken a walk in the rose garden beyond the library French doors. "They have a screwy system of leadership, won't let women into active combat roles, which delimits their numbers and effectiveness, but they're good people, good Americans. Trouble is, one of them isn't. You can kill two birds with one stone, maybe. Rescue the President and ferret out the traitor. Because the traitor won't be able to pass up this one. And if the traitor remains operational, pretty soon there won't be an Alexandria Patriot cell at all. And the D.C. metroplex is getting hot. You can't strike before dark, anyway. And I know it's one of these three men because they're the only ones who had access to the planning for all of the missions that were betrayed. I do my homework." Welles showed Holden a list of names.

"If you set it up right, he'll make some play to delay you until his people have their plans set," Welles went on. "He'll have to. But only you'll know about the tunnel's location and that you can't penetrate the tunnel anytime you want because you would be visible from the guard posts on the roof of the sanitorium. You'll know your timing has to be perfect, he won't. If you get in too early, they see you with regular optical devices from the roof. If you get in after dark, they'll spot you with vision-intensification equipment. So you have to get into the tunnel precisely at dusk, when conventional optics won't be that effective and the starlight stuff won't be operational yet. The reason it won't be operational is because they'll be looking to the west toward that road and only an idiot would risk catching a glimpse of the sun setting through vision intensification equipment and frying his corneas. Will you do it?"

"I can't risk the mission. We can use the Patriot cell in Richmond, maybe, or just go it alone."

"They already know you're in the area. They'll know you're here for this. And, if Makowski's in bed with the FLNA, they'll know where the President is. Trying it alone wouldn't make it. You know that and I know that. And there isn't any time to contact the Richmond cell. But if you give out the wrong information on how you're planning to penetrate Pinewood Sanitorium and have the FLNA waiting for you in the wrong place, you can turn this to your advantage." Holden took another look at the list of names, memorizing them.

All decisions within the Alexandria Patriot cell were handled by a democratically elected committee of seven, the odd number selected as a tiebreaker in the event a unanimous decision was impossible. One of the seven was recovering from hip surgery and was combat inactive and had been for two months. Another was an older man—he'd struck Holden as quite intelligent—who rarely left the camp for a mission. Two more of the men were involved in another raid scheduled within D.C. itself. Holden insisted that this raid not be scrubbed, even though it would reduce the number of personnel available to aid him.

The remaining three committee members were sitting across from Holden in the lead van. All seven of the committee were men. At least one of these three was a traitor.

The man on the front end of the bench-type seat, crew cut in his mid-forties and powerfully built, began to laugh. His name was M. C. Hofsteader. Luther Steel asked him, "What's so funny, Mr. Hofsteader?"

"Oh, nothin' really. I was just thinking what a crazy world this is."

"Why's that?"

"How different the Metro cell is from ours."

Rosie asked him, "What do you mean?"

"Well, now, no offense, but women in a combat role just doesn't make it for me. And with one leader, what the hell happens if he gets iced? Total rollover in the command function, total paralysis."

David Holden smiled, saying, "That's not true, really. I guess I'm the leader; at least, everybody tells me I am. But I was away for a time. Rosie took over just like I knew she would. Ran things as well as or better than I could."

"Her?"

"Yeah." Rosie nodded. "I organized all the guys into crocheting battalions and we made a big net to trap FLNAers."

Hofsteader chuckled again. "No offense, ma'am, but women don't have the balls for this kinda work."

Holden could feel Rosie tense beside him and placed his left hand on her right thigh. "Rosie was a detective on Metro PD, worked gang intelligence, vice, things like that. Balls aren't what you need; it's guts."

Hofsteader shrugged. "I see that as a real problem, all kidding aside. If we ever can get a national leadership going in the Patriots, how the hell we gonna decide on a system of command?"

"A point well taken," Holden agreed. "But I think pretty soon we're going to have to try."

Hofsteader grinned again. "I bet you see yourself as the logical candidate, don't you? Now, be honest."

"David is the best man," Rosie insisted.

Holden smiled. "If Rosie has a fault, it's being my biggest booster."

"Hell, a woman gets it put to her often enough, she'll think anything the guy doin' it to her wants her to. Women think with their pussies."

There was silence. David Holden realized he was staring at the man almost as if Hofsteader were something previously unknown in the annals of zoology and had just crawled out from under a rock and farted poison gas. "Mr. Hofsteader," David Holden said, his voice low, his words coming slowly, "I've met persons from all walks of life, all racial and ethnic heritages, many of the world's great religions, of all political persuasions. But, without a doubt, you're the rudest human being—and I use the term very loosely—that I've ever encountered."

"What?"

"He's tellin' you you're an asshole," Rosie supplied cheerily.

"I'd say that's it." Steel nodded solemnly. "And I agree, both with the original text and the translation."

"What's the 'M.C.' stand for, Hofsteader?" Rosie asked suddenly.

Hofsteader looked visibly uncomfortable.

" 'Mister Courtesy'?" she offered.

Holden said nothing, merely watching the faces of the other two cell leaders. Both men seemed quite embarrassed. Was Hofsteader trying to start a fight as a delaying tactic, or was he really just the nasty buffoon he appeared to be, Holden wondered.

Hofsteader lit a cigarette, then he said, "I know this is some important kind of deal, tryin' to get the President rescued and everything. But after this"—and he stared at his hands, the cigarette dangling between his lips just under his nose—"you and me, Holden, we're gonna party."

David Holden, deciding to play the thing out, whispered, "I only party with friends and I only fight with enemies; you're neither one, yet. So I guess you're out of luck."

"Say what you want, man, but you and me, one on one. I know you're an ex-SEAL. Don't count for shit with me. SEALs are a bunch of Navy pussies, that's all."

David Holden said nothing.

Hofsteader snapped, "Your woman's a fuckin' whore."

Rosie started to move, Holden holding her back. Steel hissed, "Knock it off, man."

Hofsteader looked at Holden. "Your woman uses a comb to brush her—"

Steel snapped, "Good God, man, where's your decency?!"

Rosie's right hand moved from under her BDU blouse. "Wanna eat this instead of your usual, Hofsteader?" The little Model 60 Smith was in her right fist aimed at his chest, Hofsteader's right hand frozen a good six inches from the butt of his Colt Government Model in a tanker holster over the left side of his chest.

Hofsteader snarled, "That how Holden here got such a big reputation? You do all his fightin' for him? And if you can't fight 'em, you fu—"

David Holden leaned forward, his hand closing over Rosie's revolver, his eyes peering out through the dark-tinted rear windows of the van. It was obvious that Hofsteader wanted a fight right now, not later; whether Hofsteader was doing it as a delaying tactic while an FLNA ambush got set up or not or whether one or both of the other two from the committee of seven was just enjoying the serendipity was another question. But to delay the fight would merely multiply the abuse. Hofsteader was evidently determined to insult Rosie until he—Holden—had no choice but to take up the challenge. Again, why?

Holden called out to the driver, "Get on the CB and give the signal we're all pulling over into those trees. Do it now." And he looked at Hofsteader. "You want a fight? Fine. We'll have a fight. A fast fight. Then we'll get back to doing our job instead of listening to your foul mouth, Hofsteader. I built ten minutes into the schedule for emergencies, like a flat tire or having to double back to avoid a police roadblock or something. Shutting your mouth shouldn't take too terribly long. All talk, no brains. That's you. So we'll see if you fight as well as you talk, Hofsteader." Holden looked at the driver again. "Stop now!"

The driver looked back over his shoulder. "Don't need the CB. They'll follow me." And he started turning the van off into the woods.

CHAPTER 24

It was her fault, she told herself. The fight was.

David was the same height as Hofsteader, but Hofsteader, not really that much older than David, had to outweigh David by fifty pounds. She'd told herself that it was flab, but when Hofsteader removed his black BDU blouse—black was sort of an unofficial uniform color for the Patriots, the American flag patch on the shoulder the important thing—Rose Shepherd realized M. C. Hofsteader wasn't flabby; he was all muscle.

She could shoot him now; it would be murder, but—She licked her lips.

David handed her his Southwind Sanctions SAS holster with the Desert Eagle, then removed his gun belt with the larger of the two Beretta pistols. He set it on the floor of the van, then stripped off the shoulder holster with the second Beretta and the knife and the two extension magazines, also setting it on the floor of the van. Steel murmured, "Rosie and I will watch them for you."

"Thanks."

She could see Clark Pietrowski, sort of meandering into a good position in case the fourteen remaining local boys decided to interfere, Bill Runningdeer already doing the same. Tom LeFleur and Randy Blumenthal were near one of the vans.

She was sorry she'd revealed the little .38 Special

revolver she carried in the Ken Null holster under her left armpit, but Hofsteader had gotten her so angry she wanted to shoot him. If he hurt David, Rose Shepherd promised herself that she would. It was something she'd never really experienced before, a man standing up for her.

Her father would have, but he was her father.

But here was David, getting into a fight for her honor.

It made her feel kind of special.

David began to unbutton his BDU blouse.

Luther Steel stepped away from the van, between David and Hofsteader. "I want to go on record as saying this is stupid. One rule. No weapons. The FLNA kills enough Americans. Loyal Americans killing each other is stupid. Period. You guys are really dumb to do this."

Rose Shepherd looked at Luther Steel and smiled, knowing full well that if someone had called his wife what Hofsteader had called her, Steel would have ripped the man's head off. And she also had the feeling that if David for some reason hadn't been there, Steel would have taken on Hofsteader.

She thought about just walking up to Hofsteader and temporarily crippling him with a fast kick in the crotch. But David's political future was at stake here, and the country's future too. David—she was convinced of it—was the only man the Patriots could rally around, and the Patriot organization needed unified leadership if it was to defeat the FLNA, even just to survive. Word of what happened here would spread. She saw the fight more on ideological terms. Insulting her had just been the excuse Hofsteader had used to provoke the fight. If she hadn't been there, he would have found some other excuse.

He wanted to show up David, defeat David. But what had David meant when he'd whispered to her, "Watch all three"?

Their shirts off, they were ostensibly weaponless— but she didn't trust Hofsteader. David and Hofsteader walked into the center of the clearing. She'd learned years ago, there was no such thing as a fair fight outside of a boxing ring and this was no boxing ring. . . .

Luther Steel watched both men mechanically, his mind elsewhere. In a moment, like two idiots, they'd start beating on each other. But that sort of behavior wasn't Holden's style. Holden, like all men, had an ego and had a boil-over point for his temper, but David Holden had never struck Luther Steel as foolish. This was foolish, delaying a vital mission for a fistfight, no matter how much Hofsteader deserved to be thrashed.

Steel had started to speak up when David Holden had ordered the vans to stop, and only his solid faith in Holden's good sense had prevented him.

Because if Holden was doing this—granted the man had insulted Rose Shepherd, granted Hofsteader seemed to be the epitome of boorishness—there had to be a reason beyond standing up for Rose Shepherd's honor. Obviously any real man would stand up for any woman subjected to such despicable verbal abuse. But why not after the assault on the sanitorium? Why now, when there was so little time?

Steel watched Holden and Hofsteader, and he watched the others, not knowing just what he did

expect, but expecting something. His eyes caught Pei-
trowski's eyes. Steel saw the same thing in Clark's eyes
that he felt in his own. . . .

Clark Pietrowski looked away from Luther Steel
and back to the center of the small clearing. Holden
and the loudmouth were appraising each other, slowly
moving in on each other.

If Professor Holden was doing this, there had to
be a reason. Double that, Luther Steel was letting him.
And because of all that, Clark Pietrowski felt the hairs
on the back of his neck standing up, because he didn't
know what the reason was. . . .

M. C. Hofsteader's left hand feigned a short jab as
he lunged forward, his right coming up fast. David
Holden stepped back and left, letting Hofsteader's right
fist catch air as Holden's right foot snapped out, catching Hofsteader on the outside of the right knee, not
with sufficient force to break but throwing Hofsteader
off balance onto the ground.

Holden dodged back.

Hofsteader was up in an instant, limping a little as
he circled for another opening.

David Holden didn't know what he expected.
Hofsteader wouldn't be about to reveal himself as the
traitor, because if he should, he'd be sealing his own
death.

But if the fight went fast and if Hofsteader was the
quisling, either Hofsteader or one of the other two men
would have to make a move to delay. Hofsteader tried
the same move—Holden thought—and Holden dodged

right this time, but walked into a glancing blow from Hofsteader's jabbing left. Holden snapped his head away in time so that the blow crossed the tip of his jaw only, but so hard that Holden nearly bit off the tip of his tongue as he fell back.

Holden staggered, a wave of nausea passing over him. He spat blood into the dirt near his feet as Hofsteader launched himself toward him. Hofsteader's right missed Holden's face, glancing off Holden's left ear as Holden staggered back again, shaking his head, trying to clear it. Hofsteader's left hooked upward. Holden snapped his head back, his right fist twisting into a straight-arm karate blow to Hofsteader's solar plexus, stabbing into muscle almost up to the wrist. Holden's left shot upward, catching Hofsteader under the jaw, driving him back. Another right impacted low and to Hofsteader's abdomen.

Hofsteader, doubling forward, rammed his neck and left shoulder into Holden's midsection. Holden sagged back and fell to his knees. Hofsteader reeled, straightened, twisted, and kicked, Holden falling back as the full force of Hofsteader's booted foot impacted Holden on the right side of the head. Hofsteader threw himself down onto Holden's right side, pinning Holden's right arm, Hofsteader's left knee smashing up against Holden's anus. Holden shouted with pain. Hofsteader's right fist drop hammered down. Holden craned his head back and away and Hofsteader's fist impacted Holden's right cheek and the right side of his mouth.

"David!" He was aware of Rosie shouting his name. "Nail him, David! Don't let him keep you down,

David! Go for his nuts!" Holden wanted to close his eyes. Rosie wouldn't stop screaming at him. "Get him where it hurts, David! David!"

Holden's left hand began to move. Hofsteader was hitting his face again. Holden's left hand found Hofsteader's crotch and Holden's fingers bit deep into the fabric of Hofsteader's BDU pants, searching for his testicles. Holden found them, closed his grip, and twisted.

Hofsteader screamed and pulled back.

Holden's right hand and arm were free. A little numb, but free. As Hofsteader rolled back, Holden swung his open hand across Hofsteader's face and heard a crack as Hofsteader's nose broke. Holden turned his eyes away from the blood spray as he crawled to his knees.

Hofsteader was on his knees, too, and Holden drew back, both fists bunching together as though he held an invisible club. He swung the heels of both fists, impacting Hofsteader on the left side of the head, Hofsteader's face distorting for an instant. Hofsteader rocked back, twisting right, and fell.

Holden was on him, his left ready to cross Hofsteader's jaw and put him out.

But Hofsteader's eyes were glassy and he just lay there, all the fight knocked out of him.

David Holden, his right arm still tingling and the right side of his face feeling odd and stinging, stood, swayed, but kept his footing.

He could hear Rosie Shepherd shriek, "All right!"

Holden closed his eyes and shook his head.

What had it proved?

Was Hofsteader the traitor, or just a rude blowhard?

He felt Rosie's hands on his arms, her fingers probing at his face. . . .

It sounded as if it had been a good fight, Clark Pietrowski reflected. Sorry no one had thought to videotape it.

But he wasn't the only one who missed it.

When he looked away from Holden and Hofsteader, he'd realized the two other men from the Patriot cell governing committee were gone.

Pietrowski moved through the trees toward where the third van was parked. He saw the two men who had left the fight standing by the van's open side door, each of them strapping on what looked like a battle or flak vest, but as one of them turned around, Pietrowski realized what it was they were doing.

"Hey!" Pietrowski knew there wasn't time to go for the police shotgun slung muzzle down across his back. So he started to draw the Smith & Wesson revolver from the crossdraw holster by his left hip. "Don't do that!" Pietrowski shouted as he brought the revolver on line.

The man who had turned and faced him touched together two wires as Pietrowski made the head shot. . . .

David Holden thought he heard a shot, but the impression was lost to him in the next instant, with the earsplitting sound of an explosion from the van nearest the road. Holden got to his feet. Rosie's hands dropped the bottle of antiseptic and the swab. "David!"

An orange-and-black fireball belched skyward, engulfing the van. Holden grabbed up the SAS-style holster from the ground beside the tree trunk against which he'd sat, tearing the Desert Eagle from it as he broke into a dead run toward the fireball.

Luther Steel was shouting something, but over the crackle of the flames Holden couldn't hear. "Rosie! Get to that second van. Get it out of there!"

Rose Shepherd broke right, running for the second van as Holden, the Desert Eagle balled tight in his right fist, stopped dead.

On the ground about fifty feet from the van, Holden saw Clark Pietrowski. Pietrowski's revolver was still in his hand, but his body was totally inert, clothing in tatters, and some of his skin blackened. Crouched beside him was Anthony Shaw, one of the other two members of the Alexandria Patriot cell governing committee. Shaw's face and left arm were bleeding and his limbs shook. He knelt beside Pietrowski, screaming, "Move and I detonate this second pack and your pal dies!"

David Holden stood stock still.

He could hear Rosie moving the van.

Luther Steel appeared at the far right edge of Holden's peripheral vision. Runningdeer, LeFleur, and Blumenthal would be there too.

From behind him Holden heard Hofsteader, sounding as if he were speaking through thick lips, saying, "For Christ's sake, Shaw, what have you done?"

Shaw, holding two wires just inches apart, the vest

that covered his upper body festooned with blocks of plastique, screamed back, "You guys are gonna sit here and wait, wait until it's too late."

Holden called out to the man. "You've got a schedule, then, when they're going to hit the President? Don't you?"

"You guys are gonna wait it out. Your man Pietrowski here, he's still breathin'. He won't be and neither will any of you standing anywhere near me!"

"Is it worth committing suicide for?" Holden asked, his voice low.

"You'd die for this lousy country, wouldn't you? Well, dammit, I'll die for what I believe in too."

Holden heard Hofsteader's voice, and it sounded as if Hofsteader were crying. "Man, what's the matter with you. This is a great country, Shaw." Hofsteader was up even with Holden now. "It's the best country on the face of God's earth, man. What are you doin'? Gimme that damn detonator!" And Hofsteader broke into a dead run for Shaw.

Shaw's hands were coming together with the detonator wires. Hofsteader—God bless him—wouldn't make it in time.

David Holden raised the Desert Eagle to full extension of his right arm and touched the trigger, the pistol already cocked, the safety already off.

The Desert Eagle bucked in his hand.

The front of Shaw's head caved inward just above the eyes and the hands sprang outward as Hofsteader tackled Shaw's already dead body and drove him down to the ground.

David Holden lowered the Desert Eagle.

CHAPTER 25

Only two vans remained for nineteen people, three of those drivers. And Clark Pietrowski, suffering apparent internal injuries, comatose and possibly dying, needed medical attention immediately.

"Randy, Tom. You're in charge of getting Clark to proper medical attention. Chester Welles should be able to help. That okay with you, Luther?"

Luther Steel only nodded, his eyes hooded, looking more angry than David Holden had ever seen him.

"We can fit ten people in the other van, including a driver, considering equipment and assuming none of us breathes too hard. Rosie and myself, Luther and Bill—"

"Count me in on this," Hofsteader murmured almost unintelligibly.

Holden looked at Hofsteader and rubbed the right side of his face. Again he looked at Hofsteader, this time at his heavily bandaged nose. "All right, you're counted in. That makes five of us. Pick the best five guys you can out of the Alexandria cell to make ten."

Hofsteader nodded, then looked at Rosie Shepherd. "The initials 'M.C.,' stand for Marion Charles." And he stood up and walked off, calling names from the group of Alexandria Patriots.

Steel said, "Do we still have a chance?"

"The FLNA must have thought so or else Shaw

and the other guy wouldn't have wired themselves up with explosives to stop us. Nobody knows about how we're really getting into the sanitorium. We have a chance."

David Holden stood up, sore and stiff in some of his muscles. The right side of his face hurt from the blows Hofsteader had delivered there.

When he inhaled, his sinuses hurt.

Rosie smiled up at him as she stood. "I love you."

Holden hugged her to him for an instant, then caught up his pistol belt and the shoulder holster and started for the van.

CHAPTER 26

They'd showered together, made love, showered together again, and Kearney left her in bed, the Smith & Wesson automatic from one of the Ford's hidden compartments on the nightstand beside her.

There was a Wal-Mart in the small town. It was all that was open besides convenience stores, a drive-through store that sold beer and wine only, and the standard American fast-food restaurants at the interstate highway exchange. It was just after five P.M. But he found the items on the list Linda Effingham had made for him—three bras, a half-dozen pairs of panties, stockings, a slip, sandals, shoes (dress and track), blue jeans, two skirts, and an assortment of tops.

The woman at the checkout counter looked at Kearney oddly as he removed the items from the grocery-storelike shopping cart. He was tempted to tell her that he was a transvestite who'd lost his luggage, but thought better of that. In a town like this he might just get arrested if she believed him. Instead he told her, "It was terrible. My wife's suitcase was tied to the outside of the trunk lid and the bungee chord snapped when we were crossing through the mountains. Thank God all her valuables were in her purse."

"Gee, that's a real shame, sir." The girl smiled back, apparently pleased at his explanation.

"Trouble is," he said, working his American accent

to the hilt, "I don't have a snowball's idea in hell—pardon the expression—what colors or anything she wanted. Just gave me this list." And he flashed the folded piece of paper out of the pocket of his bomber jacket.

"Well, you're a nice man to do the shoppin' for your wife. Lots of men? they wouldn't do that."

"You're very kind."

He paid the charges—reasonable enough—and left, the bags under his arms. The first order of business, once Linda was properly attired and they'd had a night's sleep, was to get Linda safely to her family and then return to Harrington. The FLNA and the county police for Harrington had to be in league with one another, and not just at the lower echelons, to cover up several deaths like that.

That meant the county sheriff himself.

And that gave Kearney a starting place and several alternatives. One obvious alternative was to let himself get caught.

He put the packages in the trunk of the Ford and closed it, then opened the driver's-side door and climbed inside after glancing into the rear seat and onto the floor there. The car started when he turned the key and he drove out of the lot, toward the drive-through beer and wine store.

If he let himself get caught, he would surely be taken to the Dumbrowski brothers for interrogation and killing. And he might get himself in such a bind that he couldn't get out of it alive.

So much for that alternative, Kearney told himself.

careful to stop for the town's single traffic light so he wouldn't attract the attention of the local constabulary.

The light changed to green and Kearney drove on, spotting the driveway for the liquor store.

Another alternative, admittedly slower, was to stake out the county sheriff and follow him, hoping that eventually the sheriff would lead him to the FLNA. That was iffy at best.

Kearney pulled up to the drive-through window. He rang the doorbell-like buzzer mounted on the counter extension, and after a second or two the service window opened. "Yes, sir?"

"I'd like a six-pack of Miller in bottles and a fifth of any kind of decent American port."

"Sure thing."

"Oh, and a carton Pall Malls, the red pack, and a pack of Marlboro Lights."

"Don't sell by the carton, mister."

"Then just give me ten packs of the Pall Malls. That's all right." He'd picked up Zippo fluid and flints earlier, so his and Linda's smoking needs would be seen to completely now.

He took his merchandise, paid for it, shot the man at the window a wave, and drove on. More fast food was the next order of business. He'd called the pizza restaurant at the interstate and ordered and given them a pickup time. He glanced at the dashboard's digital clock. He was bang on time as he started toward the interstate.

There had to be a way of getting next to the FLNA in Harrington without getting himself killed. He turned on the radio, heard rock music, switched channels to a country station, switched again and found elevator music. He shut off the radio.

The pizza place lay ahead.

He closed his mind to working out a solution and concentrated on his driving.

The driveway came up, he waited for a chance to cross over into it, made the turn and parked, locked the Ford, and went inside. One thing that could almost always be relied upon in the United States for a healthful and tasty meal was pizza. His order was ready. He paid for the pizzas and left the noisy, bright place filled with happy people.

In another hour or so most restaurants would be empty. Americans didn't stay out after dark that much anymore.

Again he checked the rear seat, and again it and the floor were empty. He placed the pizzas on the drive-shaft hump, keeping one hand on them to steady them as he drove with the other, hunched over slightly.

Perhaps he could combine both plans. He turned on the radio, trying station-flipping, found something tolerable, and let the music drown out the sounds of the road. He could set himself up to be taken by the FLNA or the county sheriff, then turn the tables on them and follow the survivors back. But that was risky not only to life and limb but also in terms of being able to effectively follow anyone. He shook his head, irritated at himself, wanting a cigarette but needing one hand for the steering wheel and one for the pizzas.

The motel loomed ahead. He started edging left.

It was clearly a job for two people, not one. There

was Phillip Carlysle, of course. Carlysle could get down to Harrington from Chicago.

And there was Linda.

Kearney pulled into the slot in front of their room on his second pass through the parking lot, stopped the car, and looked around.

Nothing seemed out of the ordinary.

He took the pizzas, leaving the car unlocked, and approached the door and knocked the code knock they'd agreed upon.

The curtain beside the door opened slightly and Linda smiled out at him. The door opened and she said, "You took so long."

"Careful shopper. Take the pizzas."

He left her with them, went back to the car for the beer, wine, and cigarettes and brought them inside the room. Everything was in order. Linda looked pretty, wearing one of his shirts and nothing else that he could discern. He went back to the car for her clothes, locked the car, and went inside, throwing the packages down on the unused bed and shucking out of his jacket.

He took a beer and opened it. Linda was going through the packages, holding up the tops in front of herself, looking in the mirror, then holding one of the tops with her chin while she put one of the skirts in front of her, evidently to get an idea of how well the two items went together. She smiled, seemed about to say something else, but pointed at the beer. "Oh, can I have a sip?"

"I got you your wine too."

"Oh, good—but I'll still take a sip of your beer. I need something cold."

She took a minuscule pull from the bottle in Kearney's hand, and smiled. Kearney smiled back at her. He set down his beer and started opening one of the pizzas. "You didn't seem put off by the danger of staying around me; would you like to help me? I need some bait for the Dumbrowski brothers I told you about. It might be very dangerous, but I'd do all that I could to minimize that. I've run the plays through my head over and over again, and I keep coming up with a two-person job on this."

She sat down on the bed beside him, picked up a piece of pizza, and took a small bite. Kearney opened the bottle of port and poured some into a plastic glass for her.

"I got to thinking about what you've been telling me, and what you haven't been telling me. You're English, but you're over here trying to help my country."

"Not all that altruistic, really. If your country goes, my little country won't be in such marvelous shape. No free nation will."

"Well," she said through a mouthful of pizza, "if you can risk your life for my country—and it isn't your country—I'd be a pretty poor American if I couldn't take some risks too. I mean, I'm going to be scared to death, but I was scared to death there at Siamese Shoals before you came into the bar and rescued me like that. And I didn't die, I mean, just from being scared. You know what I mean?"

"You mean if you could make it out alive from one scrape you can make it out alive from another. I wouldn't exactly bet on that, darling. But I do need your help. It's the only apparent way to get the job done." Kearney supposed she was right about one thing. It was her country.

She hoisted her plastic glass of wine and clinked it against his beer bottle. "Dark of the moon!"

"What?" Kearney smiled.

"Isn't that what spies and commandos always say?"

"Oh, always, darling. I don't know what I was thinking of."

CHAPTER 27

The entrance to the tunnel was a ground-level well-hole that had been sealed with concrete, by Chester Welles's estimate, for at least three decades, possibly longer.

But there were chisels, sledgehammers, and wedges for breaking through that, as the sound from any explosives so near to the sanitorium was something that couldn't be risked. And there was also acid.

David had told her the name of the acid, but she'd forgotten it. Chemistry had never been her strong subject in school anyway. She knew they wouldn't let her try a sledgehammer, so she asked David, "Let me pour the acid, at least."

"Look—this stuff can burn through concrete, so there's no sense risking getting it on you. Just be ready with some water in case there's an accident."

She shrugged her shoulders, resigned to the fact that sometimes it was no fun at all being a girl. She pulled the water containers, old plastic milk jugs, they'd brought along out of the van two at a time.

David and Luther Steel stood over the concrete, while two of the Alexandria Patriots and Bill Running-deer scraped away dirt and the debris of years from it with shovels.

"All right. Everybody stand back," David ordered. They all stepped away. David extended his right arm as far as he could, his right hand covered with a heavy rubber glove that came up to his elbow.

As he poured the acid, droplets of it splashed onto the leaves and dirt, smoking, but soon that smoke was obscured by the smoke rising from the concrete slab itself, with a smell like something that had gone sour in the refrigerator.

At last the container of acid was emptied and David stepped back. "We give it five minutes, then pour on the neutralizing agent and get to work," David announced.

She looked at her watch, then looked at the setting sun. They would have less than twenty minutes to be into the well shaft before they could be spotted by vision intensification optics, even though there was better tree cover than they'd anticipated. . . .

The sun was nearly down. Grayness hung over the edge of the field beside the road where they all stood near to the tree line.

David stepped toward the concrete, again wearing the heavy glove. As he poured on the neutralizing agent, there was a sound like water boiling, and there were cracking sounds from the concrete.

Goggles affixed over his eyes, Luther Steel stripped away his BDU blouse and the black T-shirt under it, taking up one of the hammers. Runningdeer, wearing goggles as well, held one of the long, very thick chisels.

As soon as David stepped away from the slab and began to close the container of neutralizing agent, Steel and Runningdeer set to work. . . .

* * *

Five minutes at the outside remained to them. Even with the added tree cover they might be spotted from the sanitorium roof at any time after that. The sun had just about set.

David's upper body, like Steel's, glistened with sweat as they took up the sledgehammers again. Runningdeer sagged down to his haunches beside a tree stump, M. C. Hofsteader beside him. Rosie brought each of the men blankets, Hofsteader looking up at her, smiling, looking odd with blood seeping through the bandage on his nose.

She just shook her head, threw the blanket across his shoulders, and went to the van for the medical kit. She returned to Hofsteader, dropping to her knees beside him. "I'm gonna change that bandage, Mr. Hofsteader. Don't try and be macho. If it hurts, swear or something."

"Yes, ma'am." Hofsteader nodded.

She could see past him and watched David and Luther Steel as they swung their hammers, like railroad workers driving the Golden Spike in some painting, their arms and chests and backs and shoulders rippling with sweat-glistening muscles, their swings timed as perfectly as if they'd practiced for the event. As Steel's sledgehammer hit the wedge, David's sledgehammer rose. As Steel's sledgehammer drew back, David crashed his downward, the hammers ringing against the wedge.

The concrete didn't split.

David and Luther Steel kept swinging their sledgehammers.

Rose kept her hands busy bandaging Hofsteader's nose.

In a few minutes or less she wouldn't have been able to see to do it without a flashlight. In a few minutes, if the slab covering the well hole didn't split—

There was a ringing sound louder than the rest and she looked up, Steel's hammer raised to strike, David's hammer swinging away from the wedge.

Steel stepped back.

Rose could barely make it out in the gathering darkness, but there was a dark crack slashing diagonally across the slab's center.

And David had put it there.

She felt her cheeks start to flush.

CHAPTER 28

David Holden, his miniflashlight between his teeth, let himself down the rope a knot at a time with Rosie Shepherd just above him. The smell of damp earth was so pervasive around them that he felt as if they were lowering themselves into a grave.

There was a ladder leading up the side of the concrete pipe that formed the well shaft, but he had no idea of its condition, hence eschewed its use. The walls of the cylinder through which they descended were caked with dirt and cracked where perhaps some seismologically all-but-unnoticed tremor had done its work, or perhaps because of the poorer quality of wartime materials.

Holden could hear sounds from above as, one by one, Steel, Runningdeer, Hofsteader, and the five other Alexandria Patriots entered the chamber and began their descent.

At last Holden's combat-booted feet touched the base of the tubular shaft. As Holden held the rope to aid Rosie over the last few feet downward, his eyes surveyed his surroundings. He saw another concrete pipe, large enough that an average woman or shorter-statured man could stand in it if he stayed precisely to the center. The pipe's interior was lost in darkness beyond the penetration of the Mini Maglite.

As Rosie dropped to the bottom beside him,

Holden said through teeth still clenched around the small flashlight, "Remember, snakes and spiders."

"Thanks a lot"—and she leaned her head against his chest for an instant. She wore a black bandana over her hair; the others wore baseball caps of various descriptions, representing everything from tractor manufacturers to baseball teams. Only Holden was hatless. Steel would be the next one down. "I hold the rope," Rosie volunteered. "You go check things out if you want. I'll be all right."

Holden nodded, taking the small flashlight from his teeth. He gave Rosie a quick kiss on the mouth and pulled downward slightly on her jaw, putting the flashlight between her teeth instead. From the front of his pistol belt he drew the larger Maglite, a three D-cell sized. He pushed the button to bring it on.

Holden shifted the flashlight to his left hand, in his right grasping the butt of the full-sized Beretta 92F. To use the Desert Eagle in the dark tunnel would have been both deafening and, because of the muzzle flash, blinding as well. A 9mm Parabellum would be bad enough here if he needed it.

The damp, earthy smell was more pronounced here, and as Holden walked ahead, shining his light along the tunnel surface, he realized why. Chunks of the concrete piping had disintegrated and portions of the tunnel were almost completely blocked with dirt and debris.

He shone the Maglite on the face of his Rolex Seadweller. It was well after seven. From the way Shaw, the man who'd been ready to blow himself to kingdom come, had spoken, an operation might already be under way to hit the President.

David Holden looked back toward the vertical shaft. Steel, Runningdeer, Hofsteader, and two of the others were already down the rope.

Rosie walked toward him, his small flashlight in her hand.

"It's going to be harder going than we thought," Holden told her. "More time consuming."

"We can't let them get him," Rosie whispered.

Holden only nodded. . . .

Holden, Rosie, Steel, and Runningdeer carried the lightweight, sturdy, and extremely portable Glock entrenching tools. The Alexandria Patriots had a mixture of GI surplus and civilian folding shovels. However many tons of dirt had fallen through a crack running the full length of the overhead arc of the tunnel was anyone's guess. But it had to be moved aside. All of them dug.

Holden looked at his watch.

Time. . . .

They were halfway along the tunnel's length. As Holden judged it, more than an hour had been consumed in digging their way through places where the tunnel had collapsed, then wriggling through holes barely wide enough for a man's shoulders, crawling, at last reaching the other side of the cave-in after more frantic digging as the newly scratched-out tunnel itself would begin to collapse around them.

Holden scratched his head, trying to shake out

some of the dirt, finally giving up. He remembered, as a boy, his mother reading him the story of the two little coal miners. He felt that he probably looked as they had, covered from head to toe with dirt.

The exertion made them breathe harder, and breathing was becoming increasingly difficult. But they kept going, Holden walking at the head of the column, head and neck and shoulders stooped, with Rosie Shepherd behind him.

They were running out of two things now: time, as before, and air. . . .

David Holden sat down, his head in his hands, feeling Rosie's hand on the back of his neck. Steel, who rarely said anything that couldn't have been printed in a children's book, snarled, "Dammit! This is the shittiest luck!"

The tunnel ahead of them was totally collapsed and there was no way to tell, as had been the case with the other cave-ins, even approximately how thick a wall of dirt and debris they needed to penetrate.

Holden looked up, his right arm, curling around Rosie's waist. "Luther. How about you and me? We dig, the others follow us."

"Okay," Steel whispered, coughing. "Sorry. That last damn ton of dirt I swallowed mustn't be agreeing with me."

"I'll go instead," Runningdeer volunteered.

"You stay back, you and Hofsteader, in case there's a cave-in," Holden said, shaking his head.

He took the Glock shovel out of the musette bag at his side and began to fold it out, not bothering to telescope the handle. If he did, there wouldn't be room to use it.

Holden faced the dirt mound and began scraping. . . .

Like a worm moving within the earth, David Holden, with Luther Steel beside him, shoveled dirt from in front of him and pushed it back along the length of his body and behind him so he could wriggle forward, only to perform the same operation again, then again, and then again.

By the time the air would get so warm and stale they could no longer breathe, Rosie and Runningdeer and Hofsteader and the others would have cleared more dirt out behind them and there would be a brief kiss of cooler, fresher air, enough to sustain them as they dug and scraped and wriggled and dug and scraped again.

Steel was saying the Lord's Prayer under his breath. Holden asked him, "What—what are you praying for? To reach the end—end of the caved-in part?"

There wasn't an answer for a few seconds, Steel presumably finishing the prayer. Then, "No, although—maybe—maybe I should. No. That—that we don't make it there too late to—to reach—reach the President before they do."

"Amen," Holden rasped through his dirt dry throat.

Dig.

Scrape.

Wriggle.

David Holden decided to try the other thing too. Dig. Scrape. Wriggle. All the while, pray.

CHAPTER 29

They reached a mound of nearly waist-high dirt. Beyond it in the light of their flashlights they saw a concrete slab. There would be bricks on the other side of this, if Chester Welles had remembered the details correctly, and if the basement of Pinewood Sanitorium hadn't been refinished.

While Rosie and Steel and several of the others held their flashlights to give him adequate light in which to work, David Holden set the charges of plastique.

Nothing fancy was required, no concealed detonators, no delays, simply something that would explode on demand. Placement of the charges was the only thing truly critical, to blow the wall of concrete and brick on the other side of it into the basement, not back toward them. If too much of the force of the explosion traveled back along the tunnel, they would be buried alive.

It was an old technique he'd learned from an instructor in his SEAL Team days, one of the times he'd stayed after hours and asked questions and had things shown to him that weren't normally shown in classes. He'd reviewed the technique with Chester Welles, since Welles's description of the entry problem suggested the technique and Welles agreed that it might work. Under the circumstances it was their best, possibly only, option.

Called the Misme-Chardin effect, what Holden intended was to drill a roughly circular hole through the wall in one explosive instant. For the purpose, aside from the plastique and detonators that they had carried with them from Metro, he had required one special item of equipment. Through Chester Welles's considerable contacts they had obtained it.

Shaped like a parabolic dish and about the diameter of a manhole cover (a manhole cover could have served the same purpose had no metal-shop facilities been available), it was made of steel armor plate and was two and one half inches thick. Fitted to its center, screwed through to the back side to be flush, was a high-tensile-strength rod made of the same material used in the fabrication of jackhammer bits, the outward facing end turned on a high-speed lathe to form a triangular spike point.

To support the object as it was fired, there was a rack. Hofsteader and Runningdeer were assembling this now with wing nuts, Luther Steel commenting that the whole thing, oddly, reminded him of putting together toys for his children on Christmas Eve.

Holden was nearly through setting the charges.

. . .

It had been a long day, but he could not fall asleep. They'd made love again, and he supposed they both felt they should take every chance possible for a moment of happiness because they might be dead this time tomorrow. Such an outlook wasn't bad for anyone, whether dynamite loader or stamp collector, he supposed. Live for the moment in case there's never another.

Linda Effingham lay in the crook of his right arm and his arm was a little stiff, so he moved her very gently, changing the position of his arm to get the circulation going. The motel-room door was locked and chained and Kearney had turned the circular table they'd eaten pizza from on its end to brace under the doorknob. If someone were onto them, short of driving through the door, smashing out the window, or burning down the motel, there was at least a modicum of safety and warning.

The Smith & Wesson 5904 lay on the nightstand beside the telephone.

Linda turned over in his arm, cuddling her face to his chest. He loved this girl, an odd experience. And tomorrow he planned to expose her to deadly danger merely so he could get the job done. But she wanted to do what she could for her country, and he doubted he could have denied her that, because he respected her as well.

Geoffrey Kearney, unable to sleep, pondered his life.

He owned a few guns and knives, a Rolex wristwatch, and various other items of lesser value. He had a car, but he went for such long periods never driving it that he sometimes wondered why he owned one at all. He had a nice flat, but he went for such long periods never living in it, he sometimes forgot where he put things, and half the time the food in his refrigerator just got thrown away because it had been there too long.

He'd been at the same business in one way or another for a decade and a half.

But for the first time in his life he felt that his chances for success were nearly zero. He would find Borsoi eventually and kill him, or whoever was Borsoi's control. Of that he was reasonably confident. But he doubted that anything he alone or in concert with others could possibly do could reverse the flow of history begun here.

The United States was forever changed, and seemed on the brink of a civil upheaval of unprecedented magnitude. If the United States went, so would go the world. Of that he was sure.

What was lacking in the modern world was leadership. There were plenty of people, indeed, to tell someone what to do, but there were few people anyone with a halfway decent mind was willing to follow, to respect, or to take as a role model or hero. Government leaders everywhere seemed all to have the same watchword, *duplicity*. The truly talented men rarely sullied themselves with politics, and Kearney couldn't blame them. The people who ran the world, on both sides, were generally men whose overriding ambition was perpetuation of personal power, not the good of the people they served and tried to lead.

He was sometimes shocked at himself, almost upset, when in rare moments of introspection such as these he realized that, despite everything in his life, he was still an idealist. Admittedly his field of endeavor was not the optimal career choice for an idealist.

Kearney, as a boy, had fancied himself going out and saving the world, fighting for truth and justice and the English way of life, a sort of London Lone Ranger or British Batman. As he matured, his perceptions changed, but not his goals. He hadn't entered his line of work because he was interested in dirty tricks, but instead because he saw it as a means of achieving his boyhood goals.

One man could make a difference, of that he was still sure. He was equally certain that, in this situation, he was not that one man.

But he would keep trying anyway.

Geoffrey Kearney touched his lips to Linda Effingham's forehead. She slept peacefully. He held her a little more tightly and, after a last glance to his gun, closed his eyes in an attempt to do the same.

CHAPTER 30

David Holden held Rose Shepherd tightly in his arms, his body almost totally shielding hers.

"Ready?"

There were eight other voices that responded, barely audible through the liquid-filled shooting earmuffs that he wore. The others wore similar ones, in the hope of saving their hearing against the terrific sound that was to come.

When David Holden was sure that everyone was in a position of shelter and had his muffs up, he lowered his head beneath his backpack and the poncho and brought together the two wires that made the detonation circuit, almost touching them to each other.

He felt Rosie breathe and move under him.

Holden hoped he'd live to have that sensation over and over again.

Holden touched the two wires together.

The tunnel seemed to pulse around him and the force of air seemed to crush his body as a whistling sound, louder than anything he'd ever heard, rose. He clamped his hands over the liquid-filled muffs, there was a roar and crashing sounds all around him, the ground was shaking on all sides of him, the external roar becoming a roaring sound in his head, his muscles tensing, his breathing hard.

And Holden suddenly realized it was over.

If it had worked, there was no time to lose. If it hadn't, time would be measured in the amount of air remaining in the small portion of the tunnel where they hid.

Holden pushed up, Rosie moving under him. He felt a tremendous pressure on his shoulders and back as he pushed his body upward, the pressure falling away then as he rose to his knees, straddling Rosie beneath him. He pushed away the empty backpack in which he had carried the explosives, the poncho catching, then falling away as more weight slipped from his shoulders.

Holden turned on his flashlight.

He was disoriented. He told himself that. The tunnel was collapsed, but that had to have been behind them. He had expected it because that portion of the tunnel was nearly completely collapsed when they'd burrowed their way through it.

He looked ahead—he hoped—and his flashlight beam seemed brighter than it should be.

Holden started to move, slogging through dirt and debris, catching up his M-16. He shot his flashlight beam back, Rosie was up, moving behind him.

Holden kept moving, stumbled, crawled a few feet, got to his feet, clambered over a mound of dirt and debris, and slipped downward.

There was a hole in the wall, the same diameter as the plate he'd fired through it.

David Holden shut off his flashlight, weak gray light, but by comparison with the darkness of the tunnel blindingly strong, emanating from what lay on the other side of the hole. His ears still ringing, Holden pulled off the earmuffs, sending a shower of dirt falling across his face out of his hair.

He stuffed the muffs into the musette bag at his left side, the bag half-filled with dirt.

Holden swung the M-16 forward, tearing off the plastic muzzle plug, blowing dust from the exterior of the action, then racking the bolt, the dust cover popping open.

Safety tumbler set to full auto, his finger out of the trigger guard, David Holden crouched and stepped through the aperture into the basement of Pinewood Sanitorium. There was ruin all around him. Wooden packing crates and cardboard boxes that had been in the path of the plate were splintered and shredded and their unrecognizable contents strewn about the floor. Bricks and chunks of cement were everywhere, clouds of dust still on the air causing Holden to cough as he breathed too deeply.

The light emanated from beyond a doorway at the far end of the room, apparently a storage area. The door lay where it had been blown down, the plate resting on top of it. The wooden door smoldering a little, the plate hot from the friction of penetration.

Holden looked back at Rosie, Steel, Runningdeer, Hofsteader, and the others coming through the hole. Holden approached the doorway.

He discerned it was a food storage area. Several ceiling-mounted fluorescent fixtures were lit, boxes of canned goods, shelves filled with more boxes, a stainless steel table, apparently for cutting large sides of beef. What looked to be a walk-in freezer door lay beyond.

Someone had to have just vacated the room, as the lights were still on.

Holden shifted the M-16 to his left hand and drew the capture-style dart pistol armed with the powerful anesthetic, releasing the safety.

Holden saw a stairwell at the far end of the room and he broke into a run toward it, Runningdeer coming up on his right, Rosie on his left, Runningdeer holding the Hawk MM-1 grenade launcher.

Holden pulled out his muffs again—his ears had nearly stopped ringing—and put them on.

Runningdeer took the right side of the stairwell, Holden and Rosie the left, an open door at its height.

Holden gave Runningdeer a nod and Runningdeer, Steel behind him now, fired as Holden and Rosie covered their eyes. They heard a whistling sound and saw brightness, despite their shut eyes. Holden counted off the seconds, then stomped his right foot hard onto the floor at the base of the stairwell, the capture pistol in his right hand, the M-16 in his left.

No one was visible in the stairwell. Holden started up in a dead run, two steps at a time. He glanced back at Rosie behind him, and Steel behind her, both still wearing their earmuffs.

Holden reached the height of the stairwell.

No one was in evidence, but in the distance, from the far end of the sanitorium—on two floors it covered eighteen thousand square feet—he could hear gunfire, and the distant rumble of an explosion.

"My God," David Holden whispered.

They were too late.

Holden safed the capture gun and shoved it into

its holster at his belt beside the full-sized Beretta, the M-16 swinging into his right hand as he broke into a dead run, the others in a wedge around him.

They sprinted along the corridor.

The corridor right-angled abruptly.

"Do it!"

Holden stepped back, drawing Rosie back as well, Runningdeer firing another sound-and-light grenade along the corridor's length.

As the sound died, Holden peered around the corner. There were three bodies on the floor by the far end, two in military cammie fatigues, another in civilian sport clothes. Holden ran toward them, Rosie beside him, Steel outdistancing him.

Steel dropped to his knees beside the one in civilian clothes. Rosie and Hofsteader checked the two in fatigues. They were Marines, throats slit, hands tied behind their backs. The civilian had been killed the same way. "This is Harlon Boyce. Point man on the President's second-string Secret Service detail." Steel's hand moved the windbreaker aside. Boyce's holster was empty. Neither of the Marines was armed, but both had empty Ka-Bar-sized knife sheathes on their pistol belts.

"Shit," David Holden snarled.

The direction from which the gunfire emanated was clear now; it came from the top floor of the sanitorium on the north side of the building, the side farthest from them. They were on the first floor now, at the rear of the south end.

Holden looked at Rosie and Steel and Runningdeer and the others. "If there's still fighting going on, there must be a reason for it. Maybe he's still alive. We go in and help the good guys, if they'll let us, but we nail the others regardless." He patted the capture gun at his side. "And the hell with these things." If they were going to knock anyone out, they were going to knock them out for good.

They started to run toward the front of the building.

CHAPTER 31

There were bodies everywhere. They had fallen errati-
cally along the corridor, in partially open office doors,
one blocking the doors of a service elevator, the doors
constantly opening and slapping shut against the body.
Uniformed Marine Corps guards, medical personnel,
miscellaneous personnel in civilian attire—probably
more Secret Service. There were other bodies, but in
fatigues with United States Army markings, most of the
faces American looking enough, but some of them hard
to peg.

Banks of fluorescent overhead fixtures were shot
out.

Steel tried his walkie-talkie, in the hopes of con-
tacting LeFleur and Blumenthal, but he could get
nothing but static. "Must be jamming the place with
white noise," Runningdeer said aloud.

There was a pay telephone booth in the hall. The
phone was modern but the booth was something from
another era, the sort of place Superman might have
used as a dressing room. The phone was dead.

As they passed an office, Rosie stepped inside and
tried a desk telephone; it, too, was dead, like the
woman slumped over it with a bullet in her head.

They stopped where the corridor took a bend. The
sound of gunfire ahead of them and along the stairs
leading upward was so loud that Holden realized that

it was likely no one had even heard the noise of the explosion with which they had blasted through the basement wall. Since no reinforcements for the good guys' side were storming over the sanitorium grounds, Holden assumed that most of the real perimeter security had been neutralized and replaced, as need be, by persons allied to the enemy force.

Three two-and-one-half-ton trucks with U.S. Army markings were parked in the driveway and on the lawn fronting the sanitorium. Uniformed personnel were standing guard over them as though nothing were happening inside. Coupled with what Holden had already observed, he was ready to shoot anyone in an Army uniform as simply being one of the killers in costume.

In addition to the three trucks there were two jeeps. Each of the jeeps was fitted with a parabolic dish similar in design and appearance to a satellite receiving dish, but for sending, Holden realized. Portable field generators were evidently inside one of the trucks, heavy cables leading between the broadcast dishes and the truck. Their purpose was clear. They were being used to jam radio communications so no signal could be gotten out of the sanitorium. The telephone lines had likely just been cut.

There was only one explanation for what was happening that seemed to fit with observable data. A spurious Army unit, in reality a team of killers, had been sent in, perhaps under the cover of guard replacements or as a supplemental force with orders warning of some sort of impending attack or a security alert. They would have been just plausible enough to get past the more distant security perimeter, to get close enough to the nearer guard personnel to kill them and replace them, and get inside the sanitorium and keep everyone chatting while the radio jamming was begun. Who might have fired the first shot, Holden could not guess. The killers, perhaps foreign nationals with terrorist background, perhaps hired assassins, were fighting to reach the President in the north wing of the second floor. Once they were successful and had murdered both the President and the Marine Corps and Secret Service personnel guarding him, they would drive their way out again under the air cover that could not have been pulled by Makowski without pointing the finger at himself as the architect of the real President's death.

By the time what had really happened inside was discovered, the fake Army unit would be long vanished.

Holden, Rosie, and the others tucked back along the corridor into an open office doorway. A doctor's name was lettered on the door and a dead man in white shirt, red tie, and white lab coat was lying in the doorway between the inner and outer office. "Running-deer," Holden exhaled, outlining his hastily formulated plan as he checked his M-16 again, "we use the sound-and-light grenades to temporarily neutralize as many of the attackers as possible while we drive a spearhead right up the middle of the stairs. You, Steel, Rosie, and myself. Hofsteader, you'll be in charge of the second element. You and your five men open fire as soon as the people by the stairs realize what's happening and begin to respond. That should give the rest of us enough time to get high enough along the stairwell that we won't be in immediate defilade. As soon as we open fire with the grenade launcher, you take Luther's walkie-talkie and switch it to PA, with the volume all the way up. Make it as clear as you can as fast as you can to the defenders at the head of the stairwell that we're on their side. I don't feel like them shooting at us too. We'll use the PA function on Runningdeer's unit to contact you when we're ready for the counterattack from the second floor. We'll hit them from above, you and your guys hit them from down here. Kind of lopsided envelopment, right?"

"You guys be careful." Hofsteader nodded, then looked at Rosie Shepherd. "And you, too, miss."

"Don't worry." Rosie smiled.

She looked ridiculous—her face was so smudged with dirt that her cheeks were the color of charcoal, and her black clothes were smudged brown. They all looked that way, Holden realized, wondering if they'd ever be clean again. But it might not be anything they'd have to worry about.

"Let's go." Holden nodded.

They left the office, moving along both sides of the corridor, Hofsteader and his men on the far side from the stairwell, Holden, Rosie, Steel, and Runningdeer on the near side.

They reached the break in the corridor.

Holden tapped Runningdeer on the shoulder as he pulled on his dark-lensed goggles and brought the muffs down over his ears.

Runningdeer nodded.

Holden gave him a thumbs-up sign.

Runningdeer stepped into the exposed portion of the corridor around the corner and opened fire, Holden and Rosie and Steel with him, their M-16s to their shoulders, firing as Runningdeer emptied the entire cylinderful of sound-and-light grenades, the shrieking whistles from the grenades maddeningly loud despite their ear protection, their eyes squinting against the light.

Holden started running toward the stairwell base, ramming a fresh magazine up the well of the M-16, dropping the spent one to the floor with Rosie and Steel flanking him.

Firing from the hip, Holden sprayed the M-16 right and left into the Army-fatigues-clad personnel near the base of the stairs. Hitting the stairs running, he took three treads at a time. Sporadic gunfire came toward them. Holden could hear nothing but a hollow noise, like the sound from a seashell pressed against the ear at the beach.

Hands groped up for him, Holden swatting away the face belonging to them with the butt of his empty rifle.

At the head of the stairs there were more personnel in Army uniforms, holding their ears, some rolling on the floor, mouths opening and closing as if they were screaming. Holden couldn't hear them.

His rifle empty at his side, the Beretta pistols in his fists, Holden fired into them, delivering head shots, neck shots, chest shots, sending bodies slamming back against the walls, blood streaking in their wakes as they slipped and fell to the floor.

There was gunfire from the roof above them, but Holden saw no immediate access.

A large room, like a waiting room, loomed ahead. Part of the wide doorway was blown out, much of the wall near it blackened. The result of the explosion he'd heard earlier, Holden realized, caused by a grenade.

Holden pulled off the earmuffs and could faintly hear the voice of Hofsteader on Steel's PA. Holden looked to Runningdeer, took the FBI man's walkie-talkie, and turned it on, hitting the PA switch. "We're friends. It appears that most or all of the attackers on this floor have been dealt with. Attention—personnel guarding the President. We're on your side. We need to reach the roof."

Rosie was beside him, putting a fresh magazine up the well of the M-16 and whispering—he was suprised he could hear her, but realized maybe she wasn't whispering—"Ready to go, David."

Holden nodded.

"Inside. Hey! We're coming in, nothing in our hands. We're—"

"Help!"

The shout came from beyond the wide doorway. Holden quickened his pace, noticing now that there were at least two streaks of blood along the floor, as if bodies had been dragged. Rosie was beside him, her M-16 at high port, Steel and Runningdeer flanking the doorway on both sides. Holden pocketed Runningdeer's walkie-talkie, calling out, "Two of us are coming in, a man and a woman. We're not here to hurt you!" But Holden jacked a round into the chamber of the M-16, left it hanging at his side as he put fresh magazines into the Beretta pistols and holstered them.

Holden's right fist closed on the M-16's pistol grip as he stepped through the doorway. On the far side of the room—it looked like a combination of conference room and waiting room, long tables with chairs along the center and couches and easy chairs along the walls, wide shot-out windows opening over the grounds at the front of the sanitorium—Holden saw a half-dozen men, four of them in Marine Corps fatigues, two in civvies, huddled together beside bullet-pocked over-turned tables and chairs, clutching their weapons although it looked as though none of them had the strength to stand.

The only man moving, as Holden drew near enough to see clearly, was one in bloodstained white shirt and half-mast striped necktie, a semiautomatic pistol in his right hand, but both right and left hands clutched over his abdomen abnormally tightly. Holden stopped moving. The other five were all dead, clearly a residual force who had held out to the last.

"I'm David Holden with the Patriots, sir. We've come to get the President out of here to safety." The gunfire from the roof was less intense now. Holden was running out of time. "How do we reach the roof? What's happening?"

The man started to laugh and cry simultaneously and in the next instant Holden threw Rosie Shepherd behind him and turned his face away. The man's intestines seemed to explode toward them.

CHAPTER 32

A precious three minutes were consumed finding the access to the roof. There was no fire escape leading upward, only downward; but there was a single metal-runged ladder leading upward to the roof through an opening barely as wide as Holden's shoulders, accessed through what looked on the outside to be a broom closet.

As Holden climbed, the sound of gunfire, though less intense, became louder, but the shooting was more or less sporadic.

Holden reached the top.

A man in Army-marked OD fatigues stood almost casually, his back to the access out of which Holden moved.

Holden drew his knife as he rose up from the ladder and moved onto the flat asphalt roof. As the man turned toward him, David Holden thrust the Defender into the man's spinal column, the body going limp as Holden's left hand closed over the mouth.

As Holden pulled out his knife and looked up, he couldn't believe what he saw.

Eighteen men, thirteen of them in Marine Corps fatigues, the others in civvies, were kneeling, hands clasped on the tops of their heads. On a stretcher to the far right of them lay someone whose face was unmistakable. He was the President of the United States.

There were a half-dozen more men in Marine Corps fatigues, in the same rank as the kneeling men, but these men lay sprawled face downward, limbs twisted at unnatural angles, faces up and down, all of them dead.

Better than thirty men in Army fatigues held M-16s trained on the still living men. One man, shorter than the rest, seemingly the leader of the invading force, was placing what looked like a fresh magazine up the well of his pistol.

When he was through, he let the slide slam forward.

There was no time for his M-16. David Holden drew the Desert Eagle Rufus Burroughs had worn.

The man pointed the pistol at the head of the Marine kneeling nearest to him.

David Holden's Desert Eagle cleared the holster on his thigh, his thumb levering the safety, his right first finger already inside the trigger guard as he started to shout, "You can't—"

There was a shot.

The Marine's head snapped sideways.

There was a second shot in the next instant, the Desert Eagle bucking in Holden's right hand as his arm reached maximum extension, the gun in the leader's right hand flying from his grasp, a splotch of red in the center of his back.

The men guarding the Marines and Secret Service personnel wheeled toward Holden's pistol shot.

Holden threw himself right, toward the metal

superstructure of a roof-mounted air-conditioning unit, gunfire ripping into the asphalt around him, waves of asphalt rising now as more than two dozen M-16's fired at once, bullets pinging off the metal.

Gunfire blasted from behind him.

Holden looked back. Rosie was running toward a chimney, firing her M-16. Steel and Runningdeer were moving laterally across the roof.

Hofsteader was just coming up from the roof access.

Holden drew, shifted the Desert Eagle to his left fist, taking the M-16 in his right.

"They've got the President!"

Holden, on his knees, crossed to the other side of the superstructure, firing a burst from his M-16. The Marines and Secret Service personnel were fighting the men in Army fatigues hand to hand, the killers firing their M-16's at point-blank range. Holden was on his feet, running toward the fight, shouting to Rosie and the others, "Get to the President!"

Gunfire tore into the roof near his feet, chunks of asphalt pelting his face as Holden wheeled toward its source, the M-16 in his right hand and the Desert Eagle in his left firing simultaneously, shooting one of the counterfeit Army personnel down. Holden kept moving and firing the M-16 into two more of the green-clad killers.

Holden caught a glimpse of Rosie Shepherd, firing out her M-16, turning it around in her hands, beating one of the fake Army men over the head with it, the stock shattering as she used the rifle like a baseball bat and beat the man down.

Holden kept moving.

Steel, his pistol in one hand and an M-16 in the other, was firing at point-blank range into a knot of the killers closing on the President.

Holden felt something tear across his left thigh and fell to his knees, rolled onto his back, and sprayed out the M-16 into the chest of one of the killers.

Once again on his feet, using the empty M-16 in his left hand like a cane, he held his right fist tight on the Desert Eagle.

Runningdeer. Holden saw him firing his Uzi, taking down three of the killers. With Runningdeer's Uzi empty, an M-16 from one of the fake Army personnel came crashing down across his back.

Hofsteader was there, firing his M-16 point blank into the chest of the man who'd clubbed down Runningdeer.

Holden dropped the M-16, drawing the larger Beretta from the holster beside his left hip, the Desert Eagle still in his right fist.

He could see the President, trying to raise himself up from the stretcher to which he was belted down. There was a pistol on the rooftop beside him. He was reaching for it.

One of the counterfeit Army personnel raised an M-16 to fire at him. Holden fired first, the Desert Eagle empty in his right hand. Holden dropped it into the holster at his right thigh as he limped toward the President.

The man who an instant earlier had tried killing the President was dying but was crawling toward the

President, a knife in his hand. Holden shot the man in the side of the head with his Beretta.

Holden dropped to his right knee beside the President, his left leg outstretched with the pain in his thigh.

"We're here to help, Mr. President. I'm David Holden."

"Holden—look—"

Holden wheeled around. One of the fake Army personnel was storming toward them, his M-16 on line with the President's head. Holden threw his body over the body of the President as he fired, Holden's upper body rocking as fire burned across Holden's right shoulder, across his right bicep, through the fleshy area beneath the right side of his rib cage. His left hand stretched out, emptying the Beretta toward the killer. Holden slumped over the President's head and chest.

Holden rolled, his right side pouring blood.

The Beretta in his left hand was empty.

He drew the one from the shoulder holster beneath his left armpit.

The President, up on one elbow, called to him. "Are you seriously wounded, Professor Holden?"

"No, sir. I'll be all right." He was bleeding a good deal, but none of the wounds were potentially fatal ones as far as he could tell.

Holden dragged himself to be beside the President, covering the President's body with his own.

He could hear the President whispering, and as Holden looked at him, there was blood coming from the corner of the President's mouth. "When he shot you, he shot me. Do this, for me, for the country—"

The President coughed and blood spattered all over his chin and the front of his pajama top. As Holden moved slightly, he realized that his left sleeve was covered with blood that was not his own. His left arm had been over the President's chest.

Holden looked down. A sucking chest wound. Holden pressed his right hand over it. "You'll be all right, sir—"

"Dying. Up to you and—to you and men like you. Don't let—don't let country—America—America—"

"America, sir?"

"Don't let—let America die. A dream. Dream for all peo—"

The President of the United States was dead in David Holden's arms.

Holden realized the gunfire had stopped.

David Holden knelt beside the President of the United States and cried.

CHAPTER 33

The telephone rang.

Rudolph Cerillia picked up the receiver.

He recognized Steel's voice. "They got him, sir."
Steel sounded as if he were weeping.

Cerillia's eyes filled with tears.

"They'll be tracing this call. Don't use your name.
Tell me everything quickly, then get out."

"About fifty men in Army uniforms. Twelve survivors from among the Marines and Secret Service
guards. All the others and the hospital personnel dead
too. None of the killers survived."

"Did he say—say anything?"

Steel's voice broke and Cerillia heard another
voice, one heard less often but nonetheless quite familiar. It was David Holden, his voice sounding strained,
pain filled.

"He told me—ahh—" Cerillia heard the heavy,
awkward sound of a man's tears. "He said, 'Don't let
America—don't let America die.'" Holden's voice
choked off. There was silence, then Holden's voice
again. "'Don't let America die, a dream for all people.'"

"God bless you, sir. I need to speak to my good
friend again."

"God bless you too," Holden said.

A pause.

Luther Steel's voice. "Yes, sir?"

"Trust no one except those whom I've told you to trust, son. Now hang up the telephone and you and those other good people with you, follow the President's last order to you."

"We can get you out—"

"I'm a—" the line clicked dead before he could tell Luther Steel that he was a dead man.

He had called a press conference for tomorrow morning. Rudolph Cerillia hadn't thought that he'd make it alive until then, and now he knew he would not.

He set down the telephone receiver and walked back to his chair. There was little time.

He faced the camcorder and pushed the pause button, taping again. "I have just spoken with eyewitnesses to the death of the President of the United States. These eyewitnesses are named in documents that will be forthcoming at a time when naming them will not be signing their death warrants. These documents were written when these persons agreed to embark upon a daring rescue mission to save the President. They were unsuccessful, but their efforts are not diminished because of the outcome, however sad.

"But the names of the men and women, the organizations, all the information I have recorded here tonight on this tape, now has the strength of deathbed testimony. I realize, as I had before only suspected, that I am the next target for assassination in order that Roman Makowski may consolidate his position and assure his continuance in an office to which he was never elected and which he has only been able to keep by means of assassination. I name Roman Makowski as the architect of our President's death this night. The information appearing earlier in this videotape will confirm that.

"May God have mercy on us all as Americans. I am Rudolph Cerillia, officially still director, Federal Bureau of Investigation."

Cerillia pushed stop.

He stood up.

Lights swept his driveway.

He went to the camcorder, popping the carousel open, removing the tape. He took another tape from beside the camcorder, placed it inside the machine, and closed the carousel.

Cerillia walked to the fireplace. He reached up inside and found the loose brick, pulled it outward. As he did so, a section of the mantelpiece on his right slid outward, revealing a niche. Inside the niche were two items: a revolver he had never registered and, hence, never been forced to turn in when he was placed under what amounted to house arrest, and a fire-resistant metal lockbox.

He took the revolver and the box of .38 Specials and pocketed them. He placed the videotape he had just made in the box, closed the box, not bothering to lock it, then placed the box in the niche.

Cerillia reached up inside the chimney again, moving the brick, the sliding panel in the mantel returning to its original position.

He looked at his hands.

They were smudged with soot from the chimney.

He wiped them clean on the underside of a sofa cushion.

There was a knock at the front door.

Rudolph Cerillia began loading the revolver as he walked toward the front hallway.

The Smith & Wesson was loaded.

"Who is it?"

"Open up. We have a Federal warrant for your arrest."

Cerillia laughed.

The door smashed inward.

As the guns came on line with him, Rudolph Cerillia opened fire. One of the five men with riot shotguns went down as Cerillia felt something ripping through his abdomen, something burning its way through his chest.

Rudolph Cerillia fell back, his finger working the trigger of his revolver one more time, unintentionally. He heard something sounding like glass breaking but the sound was fading.

He tried to make himself smile; these assassins in the employ of Roman Makowski had just validated his deathbed testimony.

Rudolph Cerillia opened his gun hand and closed his eyes.